**Praise**

"A fun read. Eileen . . . vision star add verisimilitude to her novel's soap opera backdrop, as her heroine struggles to clear her name w. . . . . . . . . . . romance . . . his . . . . . . . dunit. A . . . . . . . . . . . . . . . . . . . . . . . . . . . . . . nonfans . . . . . . . . . . . . . . . . . . . . . . . . . . . . . . . . .

*The You . . . . . . . . . . . . . . . . . . . . . . . . . . . . . . . . .*

"Through . . . . . . . . . . . Abb . . . . . . . . . . . . . . . . . . . . perspective on the life of a soap opera veteran . . . . . . cliché diva, but a warm, complex, and thoughtful single mother with a great sense of humor about herself and the 'glamorous' world she works in. . . . Readers will be thrilled with the unexpected twists and turns of the plot. I know I was."

—Peter Bergman (Jack Abbott on
*The Young and the Restless*)

"*Death in Daytime* [is] a funny and entertaining read that had me laughing out loud. Ms. Davidson draws on a world she knows very well and gives you a host of 'who done it' characters that keeps you guessing to the very end. I highly recommend the book and can see it as a movie."

—Ron Moss (Ridge Forrester on
*The Bold and the Beautiful*)

"Eileen Davidson's debut mystery has star quality with an appealing protagonist and fascinating lore about the making of TV soaps."

—Carolyn Hart, *New York Times* bestselling author

# Eileen Davidson

# Death in Daytime

## A SOAP OPERA MYSTERY

AN OBSIDIAN MYSTERY

OBSIDIAN
Published by New American Library, a division of
Penguin Group (USA) Inc., 375 Hudson Street,
New York, New York 10014, USA
Penguin Group (Canada), 90 Eglinton Avenue East, Suite 700, Toronto,
Ontario M4P 2Y3, Canada (a division of Pearson Penguin Canada Inc.)
Penguin Books Ltd., 80 Strand, London WC2R 0RL, England
Penguin Ireland, 25 St. Stephen's Green, Dublin 2,
Ireland (a division of Penguin Books Ltd.)
Penguin Group (Australia), 250 Camberwell Road, Camberwell, Victoria 3124,
Australia (a division of Pearson Australia Group Pty. Ltd.)
Penguin Books India Pvt. Ltd., 11 Community Centre, Panchsheel Park,
New Delhi - 110 017, India
Penguin Group (NZ), 67 Apollo Drive, Rosedale, North Shore 0632,
New Zealand (a division of Pearson New Zealand Ltd.)
Penguin Books (South Africa) (Pty.) Ltd., 24 Sturdee Avenue,
Rosebank, Johannesburg 2196, South Africa

Penguin Books Ltd., Registered Offices:
80 Strand, London WC2R 0RL, England

First published by Obsidian, an imprint of New American Library,
a division of Penguin Group (USA) Inc.

First Printing, October 2008
10   9   8   7   6   5   4   3   2   1

*This book is dedicated to my sister Connie,*
*who has always inspired me as a writer,*
*and now inspires me with strength and courage.*

# ACKNOWLEDGMENTS

Much love and many thanks to my mom, Charlotte Greathouse, for a lifetime of love and support. And Patti van Patten for the last six years of love and support. To my dad, who I know is watching over and inspiring me. To all of my sisters, brothers, nieces, and nephews for making my life so interesting and full. Thank you to Bill and Lee Bell for starting my career in daytime television, and to Bradley Bell for continuing it. To all the actors, crews, and production people who have given me so much personally and so much to draw from over the years! To Bob Randisi for helping me learn the ropes of writing a novel and for being so encouraging . . . and talented. And of course, love and thanks to my sons in all configurations—Paul, Duke, Flea, and Jesse—for keeping life real and *really* entertaining! And enormous thanks to my husband, Vincent, for helping me realize a dream. Come to think of it, lots of dreams!

# Chapter 1

I really wasn't all that upset when Marcy Blanchard was murdered, but that was before I knew I'd become the prime suspect.

The MBN—Media Broadcasting Network—building isn't just any building; it's monolithic, a huge, sprawling metropolis of stages, executive offices, commissary, coffee bar, wardrobe departments, and special effects buildings. You can even get a car wash in the parking lot. All of this, surrounded by a battalion of huge satellite dishes—sentries guarding the bastion of Television—can be intimidating if you're new here.

MBN has been around since the forties and is responsible for some of broadcasting's biggest hits, first in radio and then television. It started airing *The Yearning Tide* way back in the early sixties.

The basic premise of the show revolves around the loves and lives of the Benedict and Miller families in the bucolic seaside community of Hampton Heights. The Benedicts are a wealthy, not-so-nice family who made their millions in real estate. They own the hugely successful land development company Benedict

Properties. I play the character Tiffany Benedict, first-born daughter of Owen and Belinda Benedict. Tiffany has a younger brother, Denver, and younger half sister, Cicely. Tiff's the smart, kind, straight shooter of the family. Her sibs are downright nasty.

The Millers are a cop family, with little money but hearts of gold. Billy and his wife, Loretta, have two sons: Hank, a cop, and Matty, a doctor. The Millers had originally owned prime beach property that Owen Benedict (the Benedict patriarch) swindled from Sergeant Billy Miller (the Miller patriarch), thus creating a situation ripe for unending daytime drama.

There are roughly twenty-five to thirty contract players (that means regulars) on the show, give or take a few. This depends on story and budget issues. The show is woven in and around different characters but always has its core families, the Benedicts and the Millers, in the mix. It's a recipe that has worked well for *The Yearning Tide*, because it quickly became a huge daytime hit and has rated in the top three for more than forty years.

I've been on the show for close to half of those years, so you'd figure I wouldn't need identification to get in, right? Wrong. I stopped at the gate and showed my ID that day, which had pretty much started like any other. Gone were the days when I could count on simply being recognized to get in. Things have gotten a lot more rigid at the studio since 9/11, as if terrorists are going to blow up game shows and reality series. Who's to say, though; maybe that would be a good choice. Just kidding. One time I forgot my ID, but since I was on the TV screen in the guard's booth at that moment (at MBN they pipe in only MBN shows all day—very 1984) I simply pointed to the screen and then at myself—nothing. So I again pointed with more emphasis at the screen and back at myself. Okay, maybe I don't look exactly the same on TV as in real life. But it's not that drastic a difference! Is it?

But back to today. I parked the car and as I started to get out, my coffee cup fell into my lap. Further portent of a bad day. I winced, because the travel cup was a good one that kept the coffee very hot. I pulled my bag onto my shoulder, grabbed what was left of my coffee, and headed through the glass front door of the MBN.

When no one was looking, I took the elevator, preferring it to the stairs. I mean, I care about keeping in shape, but let's not get carried away! I made my way to my second home—my dressing room. Photos of my kid and some magazine covers of me on the wall, fake orchids in a vase, a candle or two. That's it. I looked at my tired self in the mirror and dumped my makeup bag out onto the coffee table. I have a bad habit of trying to apply makeup in poorly lit environments. See, even though I have a terrific work ethic, I'm basically lazy. I gave up and decided that day to let the experts have a crack at it. Off to Hair and Makeup.

My name is Alexis Peterson and I'm not a diva; I've never been a diva. Actually, I resent the term. When you hear the word "diva," you think of some obnoxious woman who happens to act or sing for a living, who doesn't have any appreciation for anyone but herself and who seems to think that only her needs matter.

I am a professional—what you call a working actress. I show up on time, I am always prepared, and I treat the people around me—cast and crew—with respect and consideration.

I fell into acting after a fledgling modeling career. I did a few B movies and guest spots until I got my present part on *The Yearning Tide*, where I have been plying my trade now for more than twenty years.

I find it odd, looking back, that on that particular day, as I was on my way to get made-up, I was indulging myself in some career/life retrospection.

Acting has been very good to me. I've been quite successful. I love to act, but I hate a lot of the stuff that goes along with it. But if I'm going to be honest—and really, what have I got to lose?—I love all the bullshit, too. It's your typical love/hate relationship. Like almost every other relationship in my life.

And then there was my marriage. Just when I was preparing myself to retire from acting, maybe write a novel, garden, you know, be a stay-at-home mommy, I discovered my then-husband, Randy, had spent my savings—and several other people's—on some investment scheme. He ended up having to leave the country or face jail time. So, presto chango, my life changed. I had to sell my very nice house and most of my very nice things because I was saddled with his huge debt, and I became a single parent. On top of all that, I was the darling of the tabloids. There's nothing more disturbing than being at the checkout counter of the grocery store with your three-year-old and having her yelling,

"Mommy! Look, that's you on the magazine! And there's Daddy, too." Of course everybody stared and then quickly looked away. Oh, screw them . . . shit happens. Lucky for my ex, he gave me my beautiful child or I would have killed him.

And thank God for *The Yearning Tide*. I not only needed to work but also loved the perks. What other job would allow me to leave home in the morning, wearing my favorite jeans or sweats or something equally unattractive, and not even—like today— bother with makeup? Most of the time I don't even brush my hair. After all, I am going someplace where they have people to do that for me.

But there are times when I'm heading down the Pacific Coast Highway and I look in the mirror and am struck by the fact that, to passing motorists, I must seem like a serial killer—only because I have a focused pout plastered on my face, you know, getting ready for the day. After all, I'm not just an actress on a soap; I'm an actress on a soap where the head writer hates me. It takes a lot of focus to face that bitch every day. . . .

Hair and Makeup . . . This was where all the *real* action and drama took place. This was the room that knew what was going on first, before anyone else. The way drunks confide in their bartenders? Multiply that by ten for actresses and their hairdressers.

My hairdresser just happens to be my best friend. Probably because of all the things I've confided in him over the years. I figure it's safer to keep him close. He's a great guy. Smart, funny, cute and very gay. He also loves color. Purple pants, pink shirts, yellow shoes.

You can't miss him. George and I discuss what "do" we're going for that day, which also depends on what other actresses are doing and the mood we're in ("we" because George and I are a team). It also depends on what kind of a scene I'm taping that day. You know, love scene, drunk scene, crying scene. George said we should do a very soft style because of all the emotion I had to play that day. I didn't know what he was talking about. Last time I looked I hadn't seen any emotional scenes in my script. Shocked, he said, "You didn't know you have a three-page monologue and lots of crying?"

More and more of my scripts, or just pages of certain scripts, were getting lost on their way to my dressing room, and I had no doubt who was behind the phenomenon.

"I'll be right back," I told George.

"Don't kill her," he said, because he knew for whom I was going to look.

# Chapter 2

And how did George know whom I was going to see? Because he—and everybody else—had heard us screaming at each other just last week.

Marcy Blanchard was a PA twenty-five years ago on the show. "PA" is an abbreviation for production assistant. They're basically gophers, but most people working on a show would be lost without them. They are the glue. They drop off scripts, cuts, revisions, fan mail, interoffice memos and all sorts of stuff. It's also a great position if you want to learn the ropes of "the business."

Over the years there has been a lot of upheaval on my show. Writers hired and fired, lots of changing of the guard. A few months ago, I heard that a new head writer had joined our ranks. The name seemed vaguely familiar. And then one day, I was on set rehearsing a scene, when I noticed, off camera, a woman standing there staring at me. Glaring, really. She looked familiar but I couldn't see her clearly because the lights were in my eyes. After the scene was finished she approached me and introduced herself. Immediately, I recognized her. Marcy Blanchard, the new head writer and a former psycho PA, one and the same.

As soon as Marcy came onto the show, odd things began happening. My lines started being cut down, my wardrobe changed—basically, it got dowdy, down-right bland and unflattering, which is not so good on a soap—and my scripts began to disappear.

That went on for months until last week, when I got so fed up that I confronted her in her office. It was so intense, I can still remember it as if it had happened half an hour ago. . . .

"Can I speak to you for a minute?" I'd asked, sticking my head in her door. "Sorry, I didn't know you were on the phone."

She looked up, saw who it was and her eyes immediately became slits. She could never quite keep the hatred toward me off her face, especially when no one else was around. I waited while she finished her call, only half listening to her conversation. Finally she hung up and then swiveled around to face me head-on.

"What do you want, Alexis?"

"Marcy, I can't do my job if I don't have the words I'm supposed to say."

"I have no idea what you're talking about," she lied.

"I know you don't like me. I heard through the grapevine that you and Gabe had a relationship. I knew nothing about it at the time. I really didn't."

Finally after months of posturing, her facade of strength fell away.

"You took him away from me," she said accusingly.

"He was the only significant relationship I ever had and you took him."

She stood up then and began crying. I mean the ugly kind—spittle flying from her mouth, swollen eyes and mascara tracks running down her face. I reached out to comfort her, and that's when she lost it.

"Don't touch me, you fucking bitch. Get away from me, you slut! I hate you and what you did to my life. You ruined me!"

Gabe Fuller had been a young actor on the show and he had a thing for me. We were both young, cute and single. We went out a couple times. Barhopping on Melrose Avenue, clubbing at Helena's. These were big deals back in the eighties. It all seemed like frivolous fun when I was a young actress just starting to feel a little success and a *lot* of oats. Our relationship eventually petered out and we went our separate ways. The guy got fired and started tending bar at one of those trendy clubs where we used to party. Sad, but true. It happens.

Shortly after, scripts began to go missing, or I'd get wrong ones. Or my call time would get screwed up and I'd be late. Things got so bad that a nasty little rumor started that I was actually a man. Now, that's just not nice. It was getting ugly. Finally, I discovered that Marcy and Gabe had been in a relationship when he met me, and he dumped her. I had no idea they were an item, but she never believed me. Eventually she left the show and went to another soap on the East Coast.

Sun rises; sun sets. Twenty-five years go by . . . and she's the new head writer on my show. . . .

What were the chances that I'd end up working for such a nut job? Well, pretty good, considering this is Hollywood.

"Gabe was the love of my life and you took him away from me," she carried on. "I never got over him. It's because of you I have no children. I have nothing but work."

That shocked me. Marcy Blanchard was in her forties; she still looked pretty good. I mean she looked the same as she did when she was a PA, but then again she was one of those people who looked fifty at twenty. And probably adding to the problem was her horrible sense of style, or lack thereof. She did have a modicum of social grace—except when she was around me—and seemed to comport herself with dignity and confidence. Who knew she'd been holding a grudge of major proportions for twenty-five years?

"So you better believe I'm going to keep making your life miserable on this show until you leave."

"That was twenty-five years ago. Grow up. Get over it!"

The glint in her eyes was bordering on crazy, but I was too mad to be put off by it. We screamed at each other some more, and I was sure everyone up and down the corridors could hear us.

"Get out of my office!" she finally shouted.

"I'll get out," I said, "but this isn't over, Marcy. If I have to go over your head I will."

"That won't help you," she said, with an evil grin. She folded her arms across her chest. "I've been given complete creative control to turn this show around, and that means writing your aging ass out."

I was so mad I couldn't see straight, but I could see her Emmy on the bookcase by the door.

Before I could stop myself I'd picked it up and thrown it at her. Not really *at* her; more in her general direction.

She screamed and threw up her hands. I left before the little gold statue landed. I remember taking a deep breath after I'd closed the door to her office and storming off down the hall.

Throwing that statue wasn't like me. I'm nonviolent. I meditated, sort of. Okay, so I didn't meditate. I *tried*. When I try to meditate I sit quietly and repeat a mantra. Unfortunately, my mantra usually turns into a list of things I have to do that day. Omm . . . groceries, cleaning, bikini wax . . . omm . . . Sarah's school cupcakes . . . omm . . . God knows I could use the stress release. I also think it would make me sound much more enlightened. Okay, I lied. I said I wasn't a diva. I never said I wasn't a liar.

But even though I shocked myself by throwing that Emmy at Marcy last week, I had still kind of hoped the thing had beaned her.

I needed a vacation.

Cut to the present. . . .

•

# Chapter 3

When I got out to the stage they were blocking scenes. Or, for you civilians, the director was showing the actors where they would be moving in the scenes. There were several sets erected on the stage. The art directors did a fabulous job designing and furnishing the sets with gorgeous antiques, carpets, drapes and light fixtures if the set was meant to depict the living room of a wealthy character; dowdy, drab furnishings were used to bring the set of the less-privileged characters to life.

If you've never heard it before, yes, everything does look much bigger on television, like my butt. Cables crisscrossed the floor, and the ceiling was a maze of catwalks and klieg lights. I picked my way across some cables, searching for the director—even before confronting Marcy (yes, again! It would be the second time in a week). I wanted the director to know I hadn't blown off my scenes for that day. I just hadn't known about them.

Cindy Pacelli is artsy and very creative. She directs a beautiful show but also keeps cast and crew there forever. She likes to express herself with her wardrobe.

"Alexis, you're not dressed. Hurry. You're in the first scene," she said in her breathy voice.

"I'd've been ready if I'd known what scenes I was in today," I told her.

Cindy's big blue eyes widened and she took a deep breath. "What? I'll have that PA fired." Cindy was always threatening to fire somebody.

"This isn't the PA's fault," I said. "I'm sure this is Marcy's work. She's been giving me a hard time since—"

"Look out!" somebody yelled. Just in time one of the gaffers jumped out of the way as a light fixture struck the floor with a huge crash, glass and sparks flying everywhere.

"What the hell?" Cindy screamed, glaring up into the rafters. "Who's up there? Whoever it is, you're fired!"

A crowd congregated around the light. I seemed to be the only one with enough sense to stay away in case a second light fell. Everyone was looking up, but there was no answer coming from above.

"Bob?"

Bob O'Connor, one of the stage managers, is in his sixties. He's smart, he's sweet, he's funny and he's deaf as a stone. Inconvenient because he wears a headset so the booth and he can communicate, yet he can never hear what they're saying. He can't even hear someone standing two feet away. So when the actors and crew started screaming at him, it made him very defensive. Partner that with Cindy's breathy voice and you had a real comedy.

"Bob!" she screamed again.

"What?" He removed his headphones.

"Get a couple of guys up there. I want to know what the hell is going on."

"Will do."

I walked over to the gaffer, a kid named Willie Something, and asked, "Are you all right?"

He looked down at one hand, which was bleeding.

"I think I caught some glass," he said.

"Or shrapnel," Thomas Williams said.

I hadn't seen him when I first came in. Thomas is one of the show's producers. He's divorced from Cindy. When they are both in the booth it gets ugly. It was a contentious divorce and they argue constantly, pulling dirty tricks on each other whenever they can. Thomas is a screamer. When he's pissed off you can hear him on the *Wheel of Fortune* set across the hall. He's tall, and his body seems to be made up of sharp angles.

"You better get that looked at," I told Willie.

"It's okay," he said. "I'll find a Band-Aid or something."

Thomas turned to Cindy and said, "You've gone too far, Cindy. Someone could have really gotten hurt, besides me."

"Don't try and put this on me, you asshole! You knew I was directing today, and you wanted to sabotage me, as usual!"

A producer in daytime TV also directs the actors. Has more of an overview of story and where to go with it, and how to play a scene. We hope.

They faced each other with their chins thrust out pugnaciously, Cindy's hands on her hips, Williams's arms crossed, both ready for the next chapter in their own War of the Roses. Nothing the rest of us hadn't seen many times before.

"I would never do anything to hurt anyone—except maybe you," Cindy told him.

"Ditto."

While they had pulled all kinds of tricks on each other, none had ever been this dangerous. I figured it was just an accident. It had to be. What other explanation could there be?

"So if it wasn't you, and it wasn't me . . . ," Cindy said.

"Bob!" Thomas screamed, as I was about to voice my opinion. "Are you getting someone up there?"

"He went to do it," a voice said timidly.

"This is going to hold up taping," Cindy said, then turned to me. "Gives you time to talk to Marcy while we get this cleaned up. But keep it down to a low roar this time. Last week everybody in the building heard you two going at each other."

I knew it!

"Isn't Alexis in the first scene?" Williams asked. "Alexis, aren't you in the first scene? Why aren't you dressed?"

"You tell him," I said to Cindy. "I'll try Marcy's office and try to finally gets things straightened out."

# Chapter 4

Still amped from the light incident—excuse the pun—
I left the set and took a shortcut to Marcy's office. If
you didn't know your way around, it'd be easy to get
lost in the maze of offices and dressing rooms, but I'd
been on the show a long time and knew all the ins and
outs of the building like the back of my hand.

Reaching Marcy's office, I turned the knob with the
intention of barging in and yelling at her, but I stopped
myself and knocked. Yelling and screaming at each
other last week hadn't helped. Maybe it was time for a
more sensible approach.

I knocked on the door, waited, then knocked again
when there was no answer.

"Marcy?"

Still no answer.

"Marcy, it's Alexis Peterson." I decided to try a new
tack. "There's been an accident on the set. Cindy needs
you."

It was a lame try. Why would they want a writer because of an accident?

"Damn it, Marcy!"

Pissed off all over again, I finally grabbed the knob and entered.

"Marcy, damn it—" I started, but she wasn't at her desk. Maybe the ladies' room, I thought. As I turned to leave I saw something on the floor. It was a long line like a velvet ribbon of . . . red. What had she spilled? I wondered. It was coming from behind her desk.

I walked around to have a look and froze. Marcy was under her desk. For a moment I thought she was trying to hide. Why I didn't know, but it made sense at the time. Then I saw something dripping from her head. It was blood, and that's what was moving across the floor, a single, long rivulet of blood.

Marcy's blood.

I wanted to scream, but I couldn't. No, wait, I'm lying again! I didn't want to scream. I wanted to laugh, like when you're at church and it's really inappropriate. I didn't hate her that much and I'm not crazy. I was just unnerved. Even more than that, though, I was very interested in the details. Where was the blood coming from, exactly? Was it congealed at all? It looked to me as if rigor mortis had not yet set in. An interest in forensics, plus Paul, a boyfriend who was a forensic scientist, was more powerful than the instinct to run hysterically out of there. A guilty secret of mine was that I always wanted to be an amateur detective. I couldn't resist taking a closer look.

I crouched down for a moment, avoiding the blood on the floor, wondering if I could help her, but she was definitely dead, and whoever had killed her had stuffed her into the cubby under her desk, with her Emmy Award—covered in blood—beneath her. The blood had not congealed yet. I reached out and touched her wrist. No pulse, and she was still warm. And I was right, no rigor.

Finally, I got it and realized exactly what I was looking at. And that was the time I decided to get the hell out of there.

# Chapter 5

One of our security guards was an ex-cop, so he knew what to do. He put the entire building into immediate lockdown, with particular attention to our floor. He summoned all the other guards and drafted some of the crew into service, as well. The rest of us he gathered on the set to wait for the police to arrive.

While we were waiting we broke up into groups—except for me. I somehow ended up standing alone, with the other groups looking at me and talking among themselves. Finally, Cindy broke away from her group—which did not include Thomas, her ex—and hesitantly came over to me.

"You okay?" she breathily asked.

I was hugging myself. I'd had two scares that day, which were two more than I was used to. Feeling a chill, I wondered if I was in shock.

"I'm okay."

She came closer, lowered her voice and asked, "You didn't do it, did you, Alex?" Something about her demeanor was weird. As if she were almost afraid to ask.

Even though I was basically being accused of murder, I still couldn't take my eyes off Cindy's prominent cleavage. Cindy and her fashion sense. (I use the term loosely.) It upstaged even an important moment like this. I forced myself to look at her two *eyes* and asked, "Do what?" and then got it a second later. "Jesus, is that what you think, Cindy?" I looked over at the other groups. "Is that what they think?"

"Well, you did have a pretty big fight with her a few days ago, and you were looking for her this morning . . . ," she said, avoiding eye contact.

"I was looking for her just to—to talk to her about not getting my scenes," I said. "I wasn't looking for her to—to kill her. God, Cindy. What do you take me for?"

She just shrugged and said, "Sorry, Alexis, I mean after your divorce, all the financial stuff, and those horrible tabloids, you've been under a lot of pressure. I just thought maybe . . ." She smiled weakly and went back to her group. They quickly put their heads together and started to talk.

My chill increased. What *did* she take me for? Probably a somewhat aging soap actress worried about her job because she had a daughter to take care of and an ex-husband who had sucked her dry financially. Was that what the police would see, too? But didn't I have an alibi? The same alibi everyone else had? We were all standing on the set looking at the same fallen light.

But *when* was she killed? We'd have to wait for the police to arrive and question us. After all, everyone in the building was a suspect.

Jesus Christ, I was a murder suspect!

I walked off, found myself a corner, got out my cell phone and called Paul.

Paul Silas and I met when I had a guest role on a TV series where he works as a forensic consultant. We clicked immediately and had been seeing each other for a few months. Paul has a PhD in behavioral science and was in private practice as a forensic specialist. His work on the show—a *CSI* rip-off that was moderately successful—took up only part of his time. I hoped he wasn't busy on the set and would pick up. My heart was racing and it leaped when Paul answered.

"Paul. Ohmigod, you're not going to believe what's happened—"

"Alexis? Slow down, will ya?" he said in his slight Texas drawl. He had been out of Austin for a long time, but the accent wasn't quite out of him.

I took a deep breath and then told him that Marcy had been murdered, and I had found the body.

"Jesus," he said, "are you all right?"

"I'm a little shook up, but—"

"Were you alone when you found her?"

"Yes."

"That's not good," he said.

"Paul?"

"Alexis, get yourself a lawyer."

"What? Now? The police haven't even arrived. Paul, do you think they'll think that I—"

"You had that big fight with her," he said. "You told me that everyone up there heard it. She hated you, was trying to write you out of the show. Think about it, Alex. You're sure to be suspect number one."

Paul was supposed to allay my fears, but I guess that little plan had backfired. Crap. I was going to have to comfort myself, as usual.

"Paul, I can't call a lawyer now. That would really look bad."

There was a pause, and then he said, "Okay, you're right, you're right." He hesitated, then added, "Look, I'll come over—"

"No," I said, "that'll look just as bad, my bringing in a forensic expert at this stage. Never mind, I'll be fine. They're keeping us here until the police arrive; then we'll probably all be questioned."

"Where were you when it happened?"

"We don't know when it happened, but just before I found her we were all on the set." I told him about the light falling and how it had stunned all of us, then had to assure him again that I was all right. "I wasn't anywhere near it."

"That's good," he said. "Okay, I'm at work, but call me as soon as they let you go. We'll go get a drink and talk."

"Okay."

"Do you need me to pick up Sarah?"

"Oh God." Suddenly, I was overwhelmed with missing my daughter. We were all we had. When her father left us, he really left us, and was nowhere to be found. Sarah and Alex against the world. I hated it when I couldn't pick her up from school myself.

I thought a second. "No, I'll call my mom. She'll pick her up if I can't do it."

"Okay, but call if you need anything, or as soon as they let you go."

"I will, I promise."

"I love you, Alex."

I hesitated, just a hair too long.

"Thank you," I said, and broke the connection.

It was what I always said when he told me that. Lame, lame, lame, I know. Even though we were sleeping together I still had a few trust issues. That's what comes from having an ex-husband who screwed you in all the wrong ways. I usually analyzed Paul's "I love yous" each time, but I didn't really have the luxury of doing that just now.

"Alex?"

I turned and saw Thomas hovering near me, his movements kind of herky-jerky. He seemed somehow . . . excited, as if Marcy's murder had filled him with extra energy.

"Yes?"

"The police are here," he said. "I mean, the homicide detectives. They want to talk to you first."

Of course they do, I thought.

"After all," he said, as if I'd asked him why, "you *are* the one who found her."

"Oh," I said. "That's right. Okay."

As I went to talk to the police, the Emmy-throwing part of our fight came to me, and I shuddered.

Number One Suspect. That was one part I sure as hell did not want to play.

# Chapter 6

The detectives had set themselves up in Thomas Williams's office, just down the corridor from Marcy's—the murder scene. I hesitated when it came time to pass that room, but the nice young uniformed policeman took my arm and said, "It's okay."

"Is she . . . still in there?" I asked. There was no yellow police tape across the doorway or anything. The door was just closed.

"Yes," he said. "We can't move her until the medical examiner says so. Come this way, please, Ms. Peterson."

He kept his hold on my arm while we walked past the door, and I had the feeling it was more like he was holding my hand than hurrying me along or keeping me from running. By the time we reached Thomas's office, he'd released me.

"Ms. Peterson?"

There were two men in the room. The older, larger one who said my name came toward me while the other man stayed back, his hip against one of the two desks in the room.

"Yes?"

The older man smiled and extended his hand.

"I'm Detective Jakes," he said. "This is my partner, Detective Davis."

Davis, who looked thirty, nodded. The fact that he didn't have even a hint of facial hair might have made him appear younger. He was one of those men whose cheeks are perpetually rosy, as if they'd just been slapped. I always felt sorry for men like that. It seemed to me they'd never really look like grown-ups until it was too late.

"We're on the LA Homicide Desk."

"Yes," I said, because I didn't know what else to say.

"Ma'am, we need to talk to you about finding the deceased," he said. "Would you like to sit down?"

"Yes, please."

Davis got off Thomas's desk, went around it and turned Thomas's chair, waiting for me to sit. He even held the back so it wouldn't roll.

"Thank you."

He smiled and I couldn't help noticing his very white teeth. It looked like he had forgotten to shave that morning, too. He released the back of the chair and went over and perched his hip on the other desk.

"Can we get you anything?" Jakes asked. "Some water? Would you like an EMT to check you out?"

"No, no," I said, "I'm all right. I know what you're doing, though. You're the good cop, right?"

They were being very kind, very solicitous. Were they playing good cop/good cop? I wondered when that would change. Why did I say that? I shouldn't have been trying to antagonize them. I guess I just didn't want to play the victim.

"No, ma'am," Jakes said, with a smile that didn't even seem forced. "I think we're both the good cops, huh, Len?"

Detective Davis just nodded. He was staring at me, not saying a word. Was that a technique of his? He almost looked like he was . . . mooning over me.

"You have to excuse my partner," Jakes said. "He usually talks more, but he's a big fan of your show, and of you. He was really excited to be coming here."

"Jakes," Davis said, embarrassed.

"Okay, then," Jakes continued. He remained standing, which made him tower over me. I wondered if it was deliberate. Then I decided to stop analyzing their every word and move.

"You seem nervous," Jakes said.

"Well, we had an accident on set just before I found the—uh, found Marcy. And then I found a dead body. I think I'm entitled to be a little on edge."

"I can understand that," Jakes said. "Could you tell us, please, what brought you to Ms. . . . ." He paused to consult his notebook, but before he could his partner said, "Blanchard."

"Ms. Blanchard's office? Why were you looking for her?"

"We needed to talk."

"About what?"

"Today's script."

He stared at me, then raised his eyebrows as if to say, "Go on."

"I didn't have a complete one," I said.

"Was that odd?"

I paused, afraid they might find my hesitation suspicious. I didn't know what they already knew. Was I the first person they'd talked to? I didn't know for sure. I decided I just had to be truthful . . . but not so forthcoming. Not at this stage.

"It was, yes," I said. "Sometimes it happens, but not a lot."

"Tell us what happened when you came to her office?" Jakes asked.

I explained how I had knocked several times, called her name and then gone in. Told them how I saw the blood on the floor as I was about to leave.

"Do you always enter people's offices that way, uninvited?" Detective Jakes asked. "When someone doesn't answer a knock on the door it usually means they're not there."

"I needed to talk to her."

"Couldn't you have simply borrowed someone else's script?"

"Yes," I said, "but I wanted to talk to Marcy about why my scenes were missing."

"I see," he said. Then he contrived to look sheepish and said, "I don't know much about your world, Ms. Peterson, so forgive me if I ask what sound like stupid questions."

"Not at all. Actually, I do know a little about your world, Detective," I told him. "I'm very interested in police work, and my—my boyfriend is a forensic specialist."

"Is he, now?"

"He's in private practice, and also a consultant on a TV show."

"*CSI*?" Jakes asked.

"No, the other one."

"Well," he said, smiling warmly, "I guess that makes you a buff."

I knew what a "buff" was. It was usually someone who was so in love with cops and police work that they made a nuisance of themselves—and, in the case of some women, slept with them. "Buff" was usually synonymous with "geek." It was not something I appreciated being called.

"Not quite, Detective," I said defensively. "I've just always had an interest in true crime books and television shows."

"Take it easy, Frank," Detective Davis said. "Give her a break."

Well, I wondered when the good cop was going to show, only this seemed like they were playing good cop/even better cop now that Davis had spoken up.

# Chapter 7

They questioned me for another ten minutes, making me repeat things I'd already said. I was sure they were waiting for me to trip myself up. Liars must do that all the time, forgetting what lies they told. Ah, but I'm a good liar. A good actress has to be. And I hadn't told them any lies, so far. At least not any bald-faced ones. More like lies of omission. I hadn't told them about my fight with Marcy, or that we didn't like each other. I decided to let others tell them that. Maybe by the time they came to me with it I would have had time to think and decide the best way to handle those questions.

Finally, they said they were finished. I stood up.

"Can I leave?" I asked. "Or will I need to get someone to pick up my daughter at preschool?"

"You have a preschooler?" Jakes asked.

"Yes."

"Yeah, my partner's got one, too. His is a boy."

"Mine's a girl."

"What's her name?"

"Sarah."

"My partner's son's name is Danny."

"Davey," his partner corrected, as if he had to do it

all the time. They didn't sound like longtime partners if he didn't know his partner's kid's name—unless it was an act to throw me off?

"Right," Jakes said, "Davey."

"May I leave the building?" I asked.

"I wish I could say yes, Ms. Peterson," Jakes said, "but I can't. You'll have to hang around while we question the others."

Damn! I wanted to talk to Paul again before they found out on their own that Marcy and I hated each other. I needed to find another dark corner where I could—

"Do you have a cell phone?" Jakes asked, as if he could read my mind.

"I—yes, I do."

"Leave it with me, please."

"Why?"

He smiled, minus the warmth, this time.

"Because I asked you to."

"I might get a call about my daughter—"

"We'll answer it if it rings," he said. "If your daughter's school needs you, we'll let you know." He put his hand out. I took my phone out and gave it to him.

"Nice," he said. "Can you get on the Internet with this?"

"I suppose," I said. "I don't really do that."

He put the phone down on Thomas's desk, then turned and looked at me as if he were surprised I was still there.

"You can go back out to the others," he said. "Thanks."

*     *     *

Over the course of the rest of the morning and into the afternoon the police questioned everyone. They also fingerprinted us, so we all ended up trying to clean our hands with water and paper towels.

Production shut down for the day and we just had to sit around on the set and wait—they wouldn't let us go to our dressing rooms. To my surprise it was Cindy who came up with the idea for some of the crew to haul out folding chairs so we could at least sit down. It was unusually considerate of her. Or maybe it was just because her own legs were getting tired. Again, people broke up into groups. The techs and camera crew sat together, some of them eventually hauling out lunches they had bought from the commissary earlier in the day. The rest of us had to make do with leftover donuts someone had brought for breakfast, because they wouldn't let us go to the commissary at this point.

Cindy sat in a group with a PA, a couple of cast members and one of the staff writers.

Thomas sat with another PA, a couple of male cast members and, I thought, someone from one of the sponsors who was going to watch us tape.

The police brought the hair and makeup people in to sit with us, so I ended up close to George and the makeup girl, Linda.

Thomas started moving around, talking to everyone about what they were going to have to do now that Marcy was gone. She wasn't even dead a few hours and I started to see why he appeared so hyper. He figured he'd be in charge of the show now—at least, until Marcy was replaced, and maybe even after that. He was probably right, too, since he'd been with the show the longest. I could see that some of the others saw his immediate seizure of power as being in bad taste. Eventually, he calmed down and returned to his seat, but I knew he wasn't done pushing his weight around.

Finally, it was getting so late I knew I'd have to call my mother to pick up Sarah. I walked over to one of the uniformed policemen who was standing at the door to keep us from leaving.

"I need to speak to Detective Jakes, please."

"Ma'am," he said, "he's busy questioning—"

"I know he's very busy," I said impatiently—surprising myself with my tone—"but he has my cell phone and I need to call someone to pick my daughter up from school. She's only four years old."

"All right," he said. "Please don't try to leave. I'll go and talk to the detective."

Why would I try to leave? I wondered. Detective Jakes also had a man standing by the elevators, and the stairwells.

The young policeman returned with my cell phone. "I have to wait and take it back."

"Fine."

I hit number two on the speed dial, hoping my mother would not have the phone turned off. She was one of the few people conscious of her cell phone ringing in a restaurant or a movie theater. Luckily, she picked up right away.

We lived in Venice, in a kind of cool, old craftsman house from the twenties that needs a lot of work. Venice is a combo of great, old expensive houses scattered right in among bad areas. There's some gang activity, but the canals, built in the twenties, add charm. Very colorful. There's also the boardwalk where artists as well as crazies sell their stuff. My mom lived in a small guesthouse out back, by the canal. It was a good arrangement. We both had privacy, and she was there for us, and we for her.

"Mom, can you pick Sarah up from school for me? I'm stuck on the set." Literally. "Something's happened. The police are here—"

"Police? Are you all right?"

"I'm fine," I said. "There's been a murder—"

"A murder? Who was murdered? How did—"

Just then my manager, Connie Wilson, beeped in.

"Mom, one second, I'm so sorry, I'll be right back. Hi Connie."

"What the hell is goin' on, Alex? Are you okay? I just got a call from a friend at LA. Marcy murdered? The fuckin' bitch deserved it, if you ask me. Did they get the guy who did it?" I couldn't get a word in. "By the way, did you read that crap script, yet? I know it's just a guest spot, and I know it's playing a cave woman on a silly Saturday-morning kid's show, but it could lead to something else! Casting wants to know if you could come in on Friday and meet the producers?"

Connie is always looking for other job opportunities for me. Some have been a little questionable. My relationship with her borders on love/hate. She's a little rough around the edges, probably from being in this business so long, and she's a real contradiction—a vegetarian who smokes two packs a day. Her gravelly voice makes her sound like a truck driver, all five feet three of her. Not to mention she loves to use lots of four-letter words. She's a good person who truly cares about me. Maybe she isn't so good at grasping priorities.

"Connie, I've been a little busy here. The script is going to have to wait. I'll let you know what's going on when I know." I clicked back to my mother.

"Mom, I'll have to give you all the details when I see you. The police want to question me now. Can you pick Sarah up and keep her until I'm done?"

"Of course, Alex. Whatever you need."

"Thanks, Mom. Give her something to eat, but not too much sugar. And please give her an extra big hug for me. Hopefully, I'll be out of here in time for dinner."

"Honey, are you okay? You sound . . . kind of scared."

"I'm fine, Mom. I just miss Sarah. Not too much sugar before dinner, remember?"

"Okay, honey. And sweetheart, whatever happens, you can handle it."

"Thanks, Momma. I needed that." She always knew what I was feeling, even when I didn't.

I handed the phone back to the policeman. He was staring. Was he a fan, or did he think I did it, too?

Just when I thought I wouldn't make it home to have dinner with Sarah, Detective Jakes put in an appearance on the set.

"Ladies and gentlemen, we have all your contact information. We know where to find you. You can go home. And please, don't anyone leave town without checking with me first."

"At last," Thomas said, getting up from his chair. "People, early tomorrow. We have time to make up."

As everyone headed for the door, Detective Jakes came over to me and said, "Ms. Peterson? Not you. We'd like you to stay, please."

"I'm sorry?" I asked. I felt butterflies in my stomach. Surely someone had told them about the fight. Now I was going to have to explain why I hadn't mentioned it.

"We have a few more questions for you," he said. "Would you come with me, please?"

"Am I under arrest?" I blurted.

He turned, cocked his head and stared at me as if I were insane.

"Did I say you were under arrest?"

"Well, no—"

"If I implied that, I'm sorry," he said. "We're just going back to your producer's office for a few more questions. No big deal. Is that all right with you?"

"Um, of course," I said, not appreciating his condescending manner. "I'm sorry."

"Did you get your daughter taken care of?" he asked as we walked.

"Yes, I did. Thank you."

He stopped at Thomas's door and waved for me to enter ahead of him. "Hopefully," he said, "you'll be home in time for dinner."

# Chapter 8

"We've heard from several people that you and the victim didn't get along very well," Jakes said once the three of us had assumed the same positions we'd maintained before.

"That's putting it mildly," I said. "She hated me." There was no point in holding back now. They'd heard it from others.

"Mind telling us why?"

So I did, every last detail, up to and including Marcy's sudden appearance on the show as the new head writer.

"What happened when she arrived on the scene?" Jakes asked.

"She was still holding a major grudge," I said. "She started trying to change my part—even tried to write me out of the show."

"She can't do that."

We both looked over at Detective Davis, who had spoken again.

"What, Len?" Jakes asked.

"They can't write Tiffany out," Davis explained, as if it were very logical. "I mean, she's almost the whole show. She's been there forever."

"Thanks, Len," Jakes said, "for that insight into *The Yearning Wave*."

"*Tide*," Davis corrected him. "It's *The Yearning Tide*, Frank."

"So you had a big fight with her a few days ago," Jakes said, ignoring his partner. "Tell me more about that."

"It wasn't a fight," I said. "I mean, you know, there was nothing physical."

"Just tell us about it," he said, "every detail, every word." He gave me a very pointed look and added, "Everything you left out the first time."

"Well, all right. I had thought if I talked it out with her, cleared the air, that we could have some sort of working relationship. As it existed now, we never talked. She sent notes to me with the scripts, and she did her best to make me look bad on the show—boring dialogue, dowdy clothes, the works. I was hoping to change that when I went to see her."

"How did that go?" Jakes asked.

"Wow," I said, "it couldn't have gone more badly."

"You attacked her?" Davis asked.

I looked over at him, surprised that he had spoken. I'd almost forgotten he was there.

"No, of course not," I said. "She started shouting at me. I lost my temper. She called me a slut and I told her to grow up, and we went from there. Everybody could hear us."

"Yes," Jake said, "that's what they said. What I'd like to know, Alexis—can I call you Alexis?"

"Sure," I said, "why not. We're old friends now, aren't we?"

"That's not exactly true," he said. "I'm a cop and you're a homicide suspect. I need to know why you didn't tell me yourself that you and the victim hated each other. Why didn't you mention that you'd had a fight just days before she was killed?"

"I didn't think it was important."

"Why not?"

"Because I didn't kill her."

He seemed taken aback by the simplicity and—I hoped—the honesty of my answer.

"You're either very smart," he said, "or very innocent."

"If I pick innocent," I asked, "does that mean I'm dumb?"

I smiled at him, trying to be charming, but he just glared at me.

"Can I go now?" I asked.

"Sure," Jakes said, still staring at me, expressionless, "you can go. I'm sure we'll need to talk again, though."

"I'll be available."

"Well," he said, "thank you very much."

I tried not to show how much he annoyed me, then turned and left.

I went back to my dressing room and grabbed my stuff. As I headed out the glass doors to the parking lot, I was instantly assaulted by dozens of camera flashes and reporters yelling out my name. "Ms. Peterson! Ms. Peterson! Do you know who killed her? Were you friends?" What an idiot. I hadn't even thought of the press! I kept saying "no comment" as I jumped into my car and slowly made my way out of the lot onto the street. Crap. Not the tabloids. Again.

# Chapter 9

I pulled up in front of my house, pissed that I hadn't been able to pick Sarah up from preschool myself.

At the top of my morning list is usually waking Sarah, getting her breakfast and driving her to pre-K. I don't really like her going for too long each day. I mean, she's barely four years old, so she's there only from nine a.m. to twelve thirty. And believe me, that makes me feel guilty enough as it is. As a single mom I try to be the one who drives my baby to school, or to the doctor or wherever she needs to go. It's important to me that she not be raised by strangers. I did have a nanny to help out when I had to be at work, or God forbid have a personal life, but after my divorce, that became too much of a luxury. Thank God for my mother. She came out from the Midwest to live with me and offer her help and wisdom. But more on that later.

Anyway, that day I got Sarah ready for preschool and loaded us both into what I call my "kid car," a 1999 Ford Explorer with a surfboard rack on top. (I have another car, though. I keep it in the garage. Miraculously, it survived the divorce that robbed me of practically everything near and dear to me, and left me responsible for most of "his" debt. It's a 1958 Porsche 356 Speedster I keep safe and covered.)

But today I had driven the kid car to take Sarah to preschool, picking up the travel cup of strong coffee from the holder after I dropped her off. I refuse to be a one-handed driver with my daughter in the car, no matter how badly I need the caffeine hit. It's not until I know she's safe and sound that I indulge myself.

So I looked forward to picking her up after school and wasn't happy when I got home. Also, I was half expecting a full frontal tabloid assault until I realized we hadn't lived here long enough for our address to become common knowledge on the Internet. And wisely I had started using a PO box to avoid such issues.

When I walked in my mother's front door, I was immediately greeted by my daughter's happy voice, "Mommeeee!" I swept her up in my arms and kissed her head. She still had just a little of that amazing baby smell left. Just enough to make me know I was indeed home. I held her close and gave her a million kisses. I wanted to fill my mother in on everything, but I needed to stop and hear about Sarah's world first.

"Liam and Jason wouldn't play with me today, Mommy. They said I was just a stupid girl and I wasn't their best friend anymore."

Sarah had been the only girl in a pre-K triad. I was afraid the boys-against-girls thing was already kicking in, even at age four. And although Sarah was a scrappy girl, the tears in her eyes made my heart hurt.

"It's okay, sweetie. You have lots of other friends at

school." I had to watch what I said. My maternal instinct wanted to teach Liam and Jason a thing or two about hurting my little girl's feelings. But before I could get too caught up in my anger issues, she shifted gears immediately, wanting to show me the butterfly she had drawn that day. Now, this kid has perspective. I spent some time oohing and aahing over her artwork until she had her fill of Mom and moved to sit on the sofa to catch up on *Dora* (you know, *the Explorer*?)

Now I needed *my* mommy.

"Marcy was murdered, Mom. In her office, hit over the head with an Emmy."

"Oh my heavens! Maybe it's time we moved back home, honey. I mean honestly. This is too crazy out here."

We'd had this conversation off and on since I was eighteen years old.

"Mom, this is my home. Our home, now. I know it's a weird life, but it's my weird life." Weak, but all I could think of at the moment.

"Now, wasn't that the woman who was trying to write you out of the show? I'm sorry she's dead, I mean that's just awful. But, on the bright side, now you won't have to worry so much about your job!" My mother's strange kind of optimism made me smile and wince at the same time.

"Unless they arrest me for murder."

"That's not going to happen, Alex," my mother said. "You're innocent."

My mom is, well, a mom. Five feet two and shrinking, very down to earth. Having "work done" means on your home, not your face. She doesn't even color her hair. She's a salt of the earth type, and I thank God for that.

"I appreciate the support, Momma."

"Can you and Sarah stay for dinner?"

"I can't," I said. "I have to go home, shower, change . . . Paul's coming over."

"Now there's a good show," she said. "He's so much better looking than William Peterson on *CSI*."

"Mother, Paul's not on the show," I said. "He's a consultant."

"I know, Alex," she said. "I was talking about the lead actor."

"I have to go, Mother. Come on, Sarah, say bye-bye to Gramma."

We made the short walk from my mother's small canal house to my larger one and I got Sarah situated with her markers and my old script pages I gave her to draw on. Then I went for a bottle of wine.

I'm not a big drinker; I'm a medium drinker, and I decided a glass of white wine would be in order.

Was my mother right—was I scared? I guess so, I mean I found a dead body today and I was suspected of murder. But it wasn't just that. I was actually feeling kind of hyped up by the fact that I'd found Marcy's body, had seen it up close. I know, I know, that sounds so morbid. But, like so many women, I have this strange fascination with forensics. Something about solving a puzzle. Maybe that's why women love to go through men's personal effects and are so nosy. We're naturally inclined to snoop and figure stuff out. Also, I was pretty proud of myself. I thought that in the end

I'd handled things well with the police. The wine was my reward. I was about to open the bottle when Paul rang the bell. I let him in and he followed me to the kitchen.

"Hey, Sarah!" he called, waving to Sarah, who jumped up and ran to him, pulling her denim skirt down over her fanny.

"Paullllie!" She wrapped her arms around his neck, and he picked her up and swung her around the room.

"I love this little angel girl!" he shouted, squeezing her tightly.

She squealed and said, "I love you, too, Paulie Wally Mallie!"

Clearly she hadn't acquired any trust issues with men, yet. She had a lifetime to do that. I watched them from the kitchen and their interaction made me happy and a little sad. Another one of those love/hate things. I was worried Sarah was putting too many displaced feelings for her father onto Paul. Maybe she needed therapy. Oh God . . . already? I turned toward the sink and looked out the window, focusing on the sun glinting off a Coke bottle floating out in the canal. I didn't like feeling vulnerable.

Paul walked into the kitchen and put his arms around my waist from behind. "I came as soon as I could."

I'm sure he could feel me resisting his embrace, but he just pulled me back into his chest. Finally, I surrendered and leaned my head against his chest and sighed.

"I'm okay," I said. "I thought a little wine might help."

"I'll get it," he said. "You sit down."

I turned and he folded me into his arms for a big, long hug. I needed that. He's tall with wide shoulders and a deep chest I can get lost in when I want to. He smelled warm and safe. I was afraid I wouldn't find my way out again. So I stepped back and sat down at the table while he opened the wine and filled two glasses.

"There you go," he said, handing me one and sitting next to me. "Can you talk about it?"

"Oh, sure," I said, enjoying the bouquet of the wine. "It went pretty well, actually."

"Good, then tell me everything," he said, leaning back, "as if you wanted me to solve it. Don't leave anything out."

I told him the whole story, leaving nothing out, and he listened with professional intensity and love—did I say that?—to every word.

# Chapter 10

"The light fixture," Paul said when I had finished my tale.

"What about it?"

"Did they find out why it fell?"

"I don't know," I said. "I didn't hear anything about it."

"I'm wondering if it was an accident."

"What else could it have been?" I asked. "You don't think somebody did it deliberately, do you? Tried to hurt or kill somebody on the set?"

"I was thinking more as a diversion," Paul said. "Something that got everyone's attention while the killer went into Marcy's office and murdered her."

"Oh my God," I said. "So it was all planned."

"Only the police know for sure," Paul said. "Unless . . ."

"Unless what?"

"Unless you take me to work with you tomorrow so I can have a look."

"Why would you do that?" I asked. "Let the police handle it."

"Alexis," he said, taking my hands, "whether you like it or not, you're their number one suspect."

"Why me?" I demanded. "Just because we had a big fight—"

"Was she married?"

"No," I said.

"So there's no spouse to suspect," he said. "How about a boyfriend?"

"I—I'm not sure. I don't think so."

"Anybody else on the show have trouble with her?"

"Not really," I had to admit. "In fact, the ratings have been up since she took over, and it looks like a couple of people who she was actually writing for might be up for Daytime Emmys."

"So she's good for the show?"

"In general."

"And bad for you, in particular."

"Oh God, the Emmy . . . ," I said.

"What about it?"

"Marcy's. It was under the desk with her, and there was blood on it."

"Probably the murder weapon."

"I forgot. I threw it at her."

"You what?"

"Last week, during our fight," I said. "I got so mad I threw it at her. Well, in her direction. I remember wishing it would hit her—" I stopped and put my hands over my mouth.

"That means it'll have your prints on it," he said, "unless it's already been cleaned. You do have a cleaning staff—"

"They weren't allowed in Marcy's office," I said. "She didn't want anyone in there."

"Did she clean it herself?"

"It's a joke around the show," I said. "She goes over everything with a feather duster once a week, but that wouldn't wipe off prints."

"No, it wouldn't."

"Damn it."

"Any chance the Emmy wasn't the murder weapon?" he asked.

"No," I said. "I got down there and took a good look. Somebody hit her with it, all right."

"Well, like I said, let me have a look around tomorrow. Who's the detective in charge?"

"His name is Jakes."

"I don't know him," he said. "But I do know somebody at Parker Center. Maybe I can get some information."

"Actually, I'd rather you didn't, Paul."

"Why not?"

"I told you, I handled the police pretty good. One of them is a big fan. I don't want—I don't need for you to go in there and save me, right now."

"Alex . . ." He shook his head. "Sometimes I wish you weren't so self-reliant. Maybe then you'd let me in more."

"Hey," I said, punching him on the arm, "you were pretty in last night. How much more in do you want?" Immediately I regretted being so flip and well, kind of gross. Paul just looked at me. I could tell he was hurt.

"You know what I mean."

I did, but it was a subject I didn't like discussing. I

knew how "in" he wanted to be with me and with
Sarah, but I wasn't ready for that. I'd been taking care
of the two of us since my divorce, and I thought I was
doing a good job of it.

"How about letting me take you and Sarah out for
a good meal."

"Oh, Paul," I said, "I haven't even showered and I
don't think—"

"I'm not taking no for an answer on this one," he
said. "Go and get dressed and we'll go anywhere you
want."

"Well," I said, "I could use some Italian food."

"Italian it is," he said. He turned me around and
swatted me on the butt. "Go. I'll sit with Sarah and
watch . . . whatever she's watching."

"*Dora the Explorer*," I said. "All right. I won't be
long." Then I had a thought. "Paul?" He turned to look
at me. "Stay away from news shows, if you know what
I mean." I nodded toward Sarah. He took a beat and
nodded back.

"I've got it covered." And he moved to the sofa.

I stood beneath the hot needle spray of my shower
and thought about what Paul had said. It wasn't anything I hadn't thought myself, but hearing the words
gave it more credence. I was going to be the best suspect the police had. That meant they would probably
be talking to my coworkers, and whatever friends I
had, eager to find out all about me. This reinforced my
feeling that I didn't need Paul to go rushing in, stirring
things up, making me look guilty. I'd take care of

things myself, but I'd save him for backup, if I needed it. I knew he'd love it if I *asked* for help.

At the moment I was giving it all way too much thought. What if the cops didn't key on me as a suspect? I was, after all, innocent. Why didn't I just wait and see what they would do, instead of driving myself crazy?

One thing about a woman and a shower. Once she gets out she's got a ton of things to do to get herself ready. That's what occupied me for the next half hour.

# Chapter 11

On the way to work the next morning I made the mistake of buying a newspaper. Marcy's murder was front-page news in the *LA Times*. I scanned the piece until I found my name. I read that part and found out the *Times*—not the *National Enquirer*, mind you, but the damned *Times*—was trying to figure out the most likely suspects. And in their noble quest they had tossed my hat into the ring. I sat outside the newsstand, stunned that a reputable newspaper would print something so inflammatory—and then wondered why I was surprised. Apparently there was less difference between the *Times* and the *Enquirer* than I'd ever thought.

My cell began blaring the Village People's "YMCA" (I don't know how I did it but I accidentally acquired that ringtone) and a couple of people getting morning papers looked at me, then did a double take when they saw my photo in the paper. I shrugged and smiled.

"Hi, Connie!"

"Al! What is up? I saw the *Times*. I know you wouldn't fuckin' kill someone. Things are getting bad at *The Tide*, but there are always other bullshit jobs out there. I mean I'm sure *The Surreal Life* would be all over you. Ha, Haaaa!"

"Very funny, Connie, and no! I haven't read the script. I think under the circumstances I'm going to have to pass."

"I see where you're coming from, Al, and that's fine, I get it, so much crap hittin' the fan for you. Besides, that's not why I'm calling. *Extra* and *Inside Edition* want to interview you. *Entertainment Tonight* has called twice and fuckin' *Court TV* wants you on, too! What do you think?" Connie was so close to salivating on her side of the phone my cheek felt damp. The prospect of her client, namely me, getting so much press was so exciting she could hardly contain her enthusiasm. I was less than impressed.

"Connie. No. No. No. I've been through this kind of thing before, sort of. You know that. I want no part of it. . . ."

"But, Alex! It could lead to other th—"

"Connie, no!" I hung up, only to find all the other people getting their morning papers were all staring at me, too.

"What?" I yelled. I got into my car and jumped out of the frying pan and into the fire.

When I got to work, there were many more paparazzi camped out in front of the studio than there had been yesterday.

"Alex! Over here!"

"Hey, Alex, tell us about your feud with Marcy!"

"How about a picture, Alex?"

Apparently, they all read the *Times*, too. I just ran by

saying "no comment." I know, I know, everybody needs to make a living, but come on! Get a life, people!

We taped some of the scenes we should've taped the day before. Then Thomas told me we'd be staying late to try to catch up.

"What about Marcy?" I asked.

"What about her? Marcy's gone, Alex, and we've got work to do. I'm here to get it done, right?"

"I mean, is there going to be a funeral? Are we shutting down until a replacement can be found?"

"Oh . . . well, a funeral will be up to the family," Thomas said. "And Marcy was way ahead on shows. We'll tape those and I'll take over as head writer until somebody else is hired, or promoted."

Every soap has four to seven writers on its staff, and they were not going to be happy about Thomas taking over Marcy's position, even temporarily. I think the last time he was doing some of the writing, *Soap Opera Digest* said our show had become "moribund." Thomas was definitely more valuable as a producer.

"You're going to write the show?" I asked.

"Don't sound so shocked, Alexis," he said. "I have written for the show before."

"Of course you have," I said, wondering how long ago we were talking about.

"And somebody has to take over," he said. "Do you know anyone more qualified than me? Huh?"

"At the moment," I said, sadly, "no."

"You better go get ready," he said. "We've got a lot of work to do. Let's go, let's go." He actually clapped his hands at me. I half expected him to pat me on the butt like a football coach.

I started for my dressing room, then stopped and said, "Wait, you said something about a family? I thought Marcy didn't have any relatives."

"That's what I thought," Thomas said. "Apparently, the police have found an ex, and a daughter."

"What?"

"Alex? Can you get ready now? We can worry about this later."

"I'm going, I'm going."

I dressed for my scenes and while George worked on my hair I talked through my confusion with him.

"Did you know Marcy had a family?" I asked.

"How would I know that, dear?" he asked. "She did *not* talk to me, honey."

"When she and I were . . . talking last week, she said I ruined her life. That she never had children, and all she had was work. Now I hear she had a husband and a daughter."

"The dragon lady? A daughter?"

"That's what I heard," I said. "I'm going to dig a little deeper when I have the chance."

If there was an ex, I thought, wouldn't he be the number one suspect? All the books and cop shows I'd seen always pointed a finger at the family—specifically the husband. But did that go for exes, too?

I finished my scenes and was free to go home. Once again I'd called my mother to pick up Sarah and see that she was fed. I thanked the parent god for a mother I was able to get along with. A lot of that had to do with being from the Midwest and not Hollywood. I didn't think I would have been able to stand a Rodeo Drive mother.

I left the studio through the back gate that connected to the back entrance of a shopping mall. I had parked there this morning hoping to avoid the press, and gratefully there was none there. Or so I thought. I heard someone call my name. I turned, half expecting to see a reporter who had somehow figured out my secret exit. But it was Detective Davis, without his partner. How did he know about my escape route?

"Detective Davis," I said. "Can I do something for you?"

"I needed to talk with you," he said, "but I didn't want to bother you while you were, uh, working."

"Your partner's not around?"

"This is, uh, kind of unofficial."

"Then it's not about the murder?"

"Well, it is," he admitted, "and it isn't. Can we go somewhere? Get a cup of coffee, maybe?"

I looked at him a little differently, realizing he probably knew my every move. Apple-cheeked or not, he was still a cop.

"There's Dupar's. On the other side of the mall. I can meet you there." Dupar's was where George and I snuck away once a month to indulge our mutual love of pancakes. "Okay," he said. "Five minutes."

I got in my car, hoping I was doing the right thing. It's not smart to agree to meet a fan away from the studio, especially if that fan is a sneaky policeman.

When I got there, Detective Davis was already seated. He stood up as I approached.

"Can I get you something?"

"Just a regular coffee."

"Not a latte with whipped cream and cinnamon?"

That was what my character had started drinking, recently, since Marcy had introduced a new set, a coffeehouse where all the show's characters met.

"No," I said, wincing, "just regular."

He looked disappointed, but went off to get it and came back with two. He set one in front of me and sat down.

"What's on your mind, Detective?"

"I just wanted to tell you," he said, "I don't think you killed that writer."

"Really? Why is that?"

"It doesn't strike me as something Tiff—I mean, you would do."

Ho, boy, I thought. He was one of those viewers who had trouble differentiating between my character and the real me. Great, one of LA's finest.

"Well, I appreciate that. . . ."

"Now, my partner, he's a different story," Davis said. "He thinks you did it."

"What?"

"I can't seem to talk him out of it. There's the argument you had, and things we've learned from other people. You know some of the cast think maybe you were pushed to the edge since your divorce and all that tabloid coverage."

"Look, Detective! That's old news and we, my kid and I, are doing just fine, really." I took a deep breath. "I mean, do I seem like I'm on the edge to you?" I had to be careful; maybe I did. Changing the subject I asked, "What about . . . didn't I hear something about an ex-husband? I mean of Marcy's?"

"Yes, there is an ex-husband, and a daughter," he said. "And there are other—look, I shouldn't even be here telling you this much. I just didn't want Tiff—you to get into too much trouble."

"Was she killed with her Emmy?"

"Yes," Davis said, "the lab has matched the statue to her wound. She was struck more than once, but the first blow most certainly killed her."

"Were my fingerprints on it?"

Davis nodded, but said, "Among others. Apparently anyone who went into that office felt compelled to touch it. We're still matching prints."

"Okay then," I said, "why should I be in trouble here if mine are not the only prints on the Emmy? I didn't kill Marcy. I would never—"

"I know," he said, "I told you, I believe you." He sat back suddenly and looked at me. It was as if he just realized what he was doing could get him into a whole world of trouble.

"Listen, you wouldn't tell anyone—I mean, nobody can know I was here—"

"Detective, don't worry, I'm not going to tell anyone," I assured him. After all, I hadn't ever told George's partner, Wayne, about the pancakes. "Least of all your partner. I wouldn't want you to get into trouble for trying to help me."

He sighed and seemed relieved.

"Thanks," he said. "I knew I could count on you, Tiff—I mean, Alexis."

He stood up to leave, then leaned over and said, in

a low tone, "I never believed those rumors about you being a man."

"Thank you," I said, matching his tone.

As he left I watched him, wondering if I had walked into a good cop/crazy cop situation.

I had a second cup of coffee and sat there awhile, trying to figure things out.

Who would want to kill Marcy, and why? There were actually people on the show besides me who disliked her. They didn't have the history she and I had, but couldn't stand her for their own reasons. I hadn't mentioned it to Detectives Davis or Jakes earlier because I didn't feel right throwing someone else to the cops, even to save myself. But the fact of the matter was, I wasn't the only one on the show who wouldn't have been torn up if Marcy turned up dead. The cops would find that out if they dug deep enough.

But if Jakes thought I did it, would he even try to dig further?

Maybe I was the one who was going to have to do the digging. Why else would Davis have come to warn me? He was telling me that I had to clear myself.

Then I remembered something. Last week, when I went to see Marcy, I had walked in on her while she was on the phone. It sounded like an argument, and it sounded personal. It got ugly—remember, I'm an expert at seeing Marcy during ugly periods—and now that I was thinking about it, she could have been talking to a man, and it could have been an ex-husband. It was after she hung up that we got into our argument. Could she have overreacted because she thought I heard her private conversation on the phone? What if the motive for killing Marcy was personal, and not professional?

Marcy had lied to me. She had an ex-husband and a daughter, and I didn't know what her relationship with either one of them was like. I also didn't know where they lived, although I had to assume the daughter lived with the father—unless she was over eighteen and on her own.

I had to get answers to so many questions, and I knew who could help me, and how.

# Chapter 12

I decided that my amateur investigation was going to have to be a two parter: professional and personal. If Marcy was enough of a bitch in her professional life to make somebody want to kill her, why not her personal life as well?

Marcy had lied to me about having family, and right in the middle of a heated argument. Why? Had she convinced even herself that there was no ex-husband, no daughter?

Instead of going home I drove to an old friend's house. Our husbands had been tight—still were—but we barely saw each other anymore, so she was kind of shocked when I showed up at her front door.

"Alex? What a surprise."

"Hello, Jean. Look, I don't want to cause any trouble. Is Bill here?"

"No, he's working," she said. "In fact, he's out of town, so there's no danger of running into him, if that's what you're worried about."

"Good," I said. "I don't want to cause a scene. Can I come in?"

"Of course."

She let me in, closed the door behind us, then turned to me, and that's when things got kind of awkward.

"I've seen the news, read the papers," she said. "It's awful what they're saying about you."

"But no surprise," I said. "It does bug me a little. I thought I had a thicker skin by now, but this is a little different."

"Look, I'm sorry about how things have gone," she said. "Bill and Randy were friends, and—"

"Jean, it's okay," I said. "I understand."

She was right; it was Bill and my ex-husband, Randy, who were friends. Jean and I had met through them, as "the wives." Ever since Randy had disappeared with most of my money, Bill would send gifts to Sarah on birthdays and holidays and sometimes just because. He told *her* they were from her daddy and told *me* he was just trying to help Sarah cope with not having a father around. I knew Bill was in touch with him. Because even though Randy was a scumbag husband, he had adored his little girl. And she him. I had mixed feelings about the whole thing. Strong ones. I hated what he had done to our daughter, but I knew she needed him. And was only going to need him more as she got older. The mother part of me wanted him to come back for her sake. The banker part of me had long since given up hope of recovering the money Randy stole from me. And now, people actually thought I was capable of murder because I had been pushed over the edge by Randy's actions. Boy, he was the gift that kept on giving. I hoped that he'd ended up someplace where my money was hard to spend. Or maybe he was in South America and had been the innocent victim of a coup.

"I'm actually here to see Will," I said.

"Will?" She was wondering why I wanted to see her fifteen-year-old son. He was probably sixteen by now. We all knew that Will had a terrible crush on me, but what I'd never told anyone was that I'd always found him kind of creepy. He was, however, a computer whiz, and I needed one, at the moment.

"Y-yes, he's home. He's in his room. Why do you want to see Will?"

"I need some information," I said.

"From Will?"

"From Will's computer."

Suddenly she relaxed.

"Oh, well, he is a genius on that thing. He can find out anything you want."

"Can I go up to his room? We can leave the door open, if you like." I didn't want her to think I would try to take advantage of her son or do something strange.

"Oh, don't be silly," she said, touching my arm, then pulling her hand away quickly, as if the touch might have been a betrayal of our husbands' friendship. "I'll take you up."

When his mother knocked on the door and we entered, he leaped to his feet and gaped at me. Naturally, Will was surprised to see me. Since I'd always found his crush on me kind of icky, I'd never really been very friendly to him.

"Will, Alex is here to see you."

"Hello, Mrs. Peterson," he said respectfully.

I have to say I always suspected Will of being an Eddie Haskell type—polite in front of adults but something else again around his peers. Or me.

"Hello, Will," I said. "I need help with something I know you can handle—computer stuff."

I looked around the room and saw three computer screens in view. The computers themselves were out of sight, probably under a table or behind a stack of books.

"I have some things to do downstairs," Jean said. "I'll leave you to it."

As Jean walked out, she left the door open. I watched her, then turned to look at Will, who was staring at me, kind of glassy-eyed. I wondered if his mother and I had walked in on something weird. Behind him a computer screen had gone blank. I was sure there had been something on it.

"Um, what can I do for you, Mrs. Peterson?"

"Will, I need to find out information about . . . well, some people."

"Personal information?"

"Yes, can you do that?"

"I can run a Google search," he said, "or Yahoo, or any number of search engines. What do you want to know?"

"Can I have something to write on?" I asked.

He turned around to pick up a pad and pencil from his desk. In doing so he nudged the computer mouse, and the screen came on. I had enough time to see an impressive pair of naked boobs before he hurriedly touched something that made the screen go blank again. When he turned to me, his face was very red and he was sweating. I acted like I hadn't seen a thing.

"H-here."

I took the pad and wrote down Marcy's full name.

"I need to find out about this woman's family," I said. "I mean, if she has any, where they are, stuff like that."

"Sure," he said. "I might have to cut a few corners."

"Would that get you into trouble?" I asked. "I don't want to get you into any trouble."

"Oh, don't worry about me, Mrs. Peterson," he said. "I can protect myself—online, I mean."

"I'll bet you can." Will was turning out to be less creepy—despite the Girls Gone Wild pictures. He was actually cute, trying to impress me.

"I can pay you—"

"Oh, no," he said. "I don't want any money. I like having jobs to do on the Web. I'll do it for you for nothing."

"Well," I said, "maybe you'd like to come to the set sometime?"

His eyes lit up.

"That'd be awesome!"

"Okay, then," I said. "That'll be your payment. Um, how soon can you get this for me?"

"Do you have a computer?"

"I do," I admitted, "but I'm not all that computer literate."

"That's okay," he said. "I can just send you the information in an e-mail."

He wrote his private number down and handed it to me.

"Thank you, Will."

"Sure, Mrs. Peterson."

"And why don't you just call me Alex from now on, huh?"

"Wow," he said. "Thanks, Mrs. Peterson."

"No," I said, "thank you, Will."

Impulsively, I leaned over and kissed his cheek. He turned beet red, and I got out of there before I embarrassed him some more.

When I went back downstairs Jean came out of the kitchen.

"Everything okay?"

"Fine," I said. "Will's just going to do some work for me."

"Well," she said, "you couldn't ask for anybody better." She was so proud.

"I know that, Jean," I said. "That's why I came to see him."

She walked me to the door and stammered, "Um, we'll have to—you know, get together, um, sometime. You know, after all this murder stuff blows over."

I almost asked her if she had heard from Randy. But I stopped myself. This wasn't the right time or place. Instead I said, "That'd be nice, Jean," and then to take the onus off her I added, "I'll call you."

# Chapter 13

I couldn't do any more work on my plan that evening. When I got home, Sarah was running a slight fever. I had her sleep in my bed so I could check on her all night. Of course, I got about two hours' sleep in the process.

Sleep deprivation and I are old friends. I hauled myself out of bed in the morning, gave my little and still-hot sleeping beauty a kiss on the forehead and went in to work early to finish catching up on scenes. My mom came over to stay with Sarah.

Because we were behind, there were more cast members around than usual, and I felt myself looking at them all as potential suspects.

Cindy Pacelli had asked me on the day of the murder if I'd done it, but did that necessarily mean she hadn't? Marcy had been openly critical of the way Cindy dressed at work, calling her attire too "revealing." In return, Cindy went around saying Marcy dressed like an "old maid." I wondered if anyone had told the detectives about *that*.

Thomas thought Marcy had been given too much power by the network. He didn't like it, but there

wasn't much he could do. He couldn't be too sad
about her murder, then. Total control would be turned
back over to him. He was already reveling in it. Was
that something he would have killed for?

As I came in contact with other cast members during the day, I tried to figure out what motive they
might each have had to kill Marcy.

I talked that over with the only person I could—
George.

"Either one of them could've done it," I said, starting with Cindy and Thomas.

He looked at me in the mirror and asked, "Weren't
they on the set like you were when the light fell?"

"Yeah, I guess they were," I said, "but then a lot of
people were around. Somebody could have slipped
out to kill her, and then snuck back in during the
commotion."

"Is that what the police are thinking about you?"
George asked.

"I suppose so," I said. "I'm the only one who had a
screaming match with her, one that everyone heard."

"But you're not the only one who had problems
with her," he said. "Not by a long shot. And I mean,
even more people than just Cindy and Thomas."

"George," I said, eyeing him in the mirror, "what do
you know?"

"Just little things I hear, darling," he said, smooth-
ing the sleeve of his orange silk shirt. "And little things
Linda hears when she's got some of you in her chair."

Linda was Makeup, and I knew Hair and Makeup
shared a lot of gossip.

"You have to give, George," I told him. "Give till it hurts."

Before he could respond, my cell sang out, "Young men!" George looked at me questioningly. "Don't ask. What, Connie?"

"Don't hang up, Al, okay? Listen up. You are hot, hot, hot and we have to strike now!" Again with this?

"Connie, I'm hot because people think I'm a killer! I'm not interested in capitalizing on that!" She was starting to bug me.

"Al, this is different. It's a lead fuckin' role. Yes, it's a B, maybe B-minus movie and a little violent. But a nice fuckin' juicy role."

I hesitated but, ever the actress, I bit.

"How violent?"

"Now just listen. The film is being done by fuckin' Quentin Tarantino! Well, not exactly Tarantino . . . more like an old classmate of his from film school. But they have very similar directing styles. And your character will have to kill a few people. With a hatchet. One's your frickin' boss in the movie! That's kind of fun, right? Oh, and just a little bit of nudity. Wait, wait, it could lead—"

I pressed END with every fiber of my being. Connie had clearly lost her mind. I was about to complain to George about the absurdity of the whole thing when Amanda Ballard came in, whining that her hair just would not behave.

Amanda's a pretty thirtysomething who plays Tiffany's younger half sister, Cicely. Amanda was in a soap opera love triangle along with a good-looking, hunky guy by the name of Roman Stroud and another pretty actress named Hannah Varga. Things started getting interesting when Hannah took it upon herself to get a boob job. Not unheard of in Hollywood. Now, Amanda had a "slightly" competitive nature, and like a lot of actresses and actors, she's insecure. It kind of goes with the territory. She was used to being the "hot girl" on the show, so she decided she'd get her boobs worked over, too. Actually, she had already had one procedure. So, she went bigger. Then Hannah, not to be outdone, went even bigger. This went on for a while, until both women started looking like two toothpicks with martini olives attached. Eventually, Hannah was let go and Amanda was left with a pair of enormous bazoongas!

"I'm done here," I said, getting out of the chair. "Go ahead and take care of her, George."

"Thanks, Alex," Amanda said, taking my place. "You're a sweetie."

I was about to leave when I noticed George rolling his eyes at me. Apparently, some of the gossip he and Linda had shared had something to do with Amanda. I decided to have a little visit.

I sat in the empty chair next to Boobzilla.

"Pretty terrible what happened to Marcy, huh?" I asked.

"I guess," she said.

"I mean, what a way to go, stuffed under her desk with her Emmy?"

She turned her head to look at me. Then her eyes widened and she said, "Omigod, that's right, you found her, didn't you?" It was clear she already knew all the facts. I wondered why she was giving me the big eyes.

"Yes, I did."

If I had been looking for sympathy, I was barking up the wrong tree.

"Well, that couldn't've been too bad for you," she said, going back to the mirror.

"What do you mean?"

"Everybody knows you and she hated each other," Amanda said. "I mean, we all heard the scream fest you had last week."

"That was just . . . a discussion."

"Yeah, right."

"Well, you and Marcy weren't exactly tight," I pointed out.

She looked at me again.

"What do you mean?"

"Just that . . . things get around." I shrugged. "You know. Rumors."

"Look," she said, anxiously, "none of that stuff was true. Marcy and me, we were just—"

"Yes?"

Her eyes narrowed suspiciously as she turned her head to look at me again.

"What are you getting at, Alex?"

"I'm just making conversation."

"No," Amanda said, "you're worried that the cops suspect you because somebody . . . everybody must've told them about you and Marcy."

"And nobody told them about *you* and Marcy?"

"There was nothing to tell." She looked back into

the mirror at George and said, "That's good enough, George, thanks."

"But I didn't do—" George said, as she got out of the chair.

"You were on the set that day, weren't you, Amanda?" I asked.

"You should know," she said. "We were supposed to do that big emotional scene together that day, only you showed up late."

The scene Marcy had kept me from knowing anything about.

"Look, Alex, Marcy was a bitch, pure and simple," Amanda said. "We all know that, but we also know you were the one she was trying to write off the show. You're the one everybody thinks killed her."

"Amanda—"

She stormed out of the room, leaving me and George looking at each other.

"If you're gonna play amateur detective," he said, pointing with his comb at the door Amanda had just gone through, "you're gonna have to be more subtle, or that's what you're gonna run up against."

"I can see I'm going to have to play it a lot cooler," I said. "George, what was with the rolling eyes? What do you know?"

"I just heard from Linda that Amanda and Marcy were having . . . problems."

"What kind of problems?"

He shrugged.

"I guess you're going to have to ask Linda about that," he said.

That wouldn't be a problem. Linda loved to gossip

while working on your makeup. I only wondered what she had to say about me when I wasn't around.

"I'll see you later, George."

"You be careful, girlfriend," he said. "If you need any help, you just call me, you hear? You can count on me."

He meant every word, which made me feel warm for just a moment.

"I know I can, George."

# Chapter 14

I wasn't able to get Linda alone that morning. We both had too much work to do. It was just as well. After my failure with Amanda I knew I was going to have to figure out a new—what? Bedside manner? What did cops call it? A new interrogation technique?

They had brought in Sammy Horner, aka Timber, to help us catch up. As a director he's a quick one. He saves the show lots of overtime dollars. Only one problem: He has a large belly and it affects his balance. He tends to fall over a lot. But he saves so much money the execs are reticent to let him go. Now they needed him to help us get back on schedule.

I decided to try to talk to Sammy about Marcy's death. I doubted he'd kill her over one lost show a week, but I've watched enough crime TV and read enough books—fiction and nonfiction—to know that people kill for the strangest—and smallest—reasons.

Toward the end of the day I managed to spot him going into the commissary.

Here's where the really scary part of the day happens for me. You have to be brave—very brave—to face the commissary chef, Jose. Do you remember the

Soup Nazi on *Seinfeld*? Jose is a short-order cook with a psycho-killer look that scares the crap out of me. He's better known as Jose the Horrible. I'm a strong woman. I can hold my own with narcissistic leading men, ego-driven writers and sociopath ex-husbands. But our food fascist strikes terror deep into my heart. I have been known to accept, with a smile, something I never ordered, just because I was afraid to face the wrath of Jose the Terrible. Obviously, it was entirely my fault that I hadn't spoken clearly enough.

This time, to be on the safe side, I just got a cup of coffee. Coffee was self-serve and not confrontational. I couldn't handle any more confrontation. Not just yet.

Sammy had taken a table alone; the burger plate sat in front of him.

"Can I join you?" I asked, standing by the small table with my coffee.

Now, I knew Sammy pretty well and knew that he always sat at a smaller table because he did not want people to join him. Apparently, on this day, he didn't quite know how to say no. And besides, I was only holding coffee. How long could it take me to finish it?

"Sure, why not?" he said.

"Terrible thing about Marcy, isn't it?"

"Yeah, really terrible," Sammy said. "It's because of that bitch my workload was cut. So now they need ol' Timber to help them catch up. I'd like to tell 'em to go fuck themselves, but . . ."

But he needed the job.

"I meant, about her getting killed."

"I know what you meant, Alex," Sammy said. He leaned over to take a bite of his burger and his belly bumped the table, making it rock. I grabbed my coffee before it could spill.

"Sorry," he muttered.

"Aren't you upset?" I asked.

"Let's not pretend either one of us is upset she's dead, Alex. She was a true bitch, in the best and worst sense of that word. You know that better than anyone else. She had it out for you from day one. That, coupled with everything else you've gone through in the last two years. Nobody'd blame you if you—" He stopped short.

"If I what?"

Sammy chewed, swallowed and said, "If you killed her."

"Jesus, Sammy," I said. "I didn't kill her. I mean . . . I didn't."

"I didn't say you did," he replied. "I just said nobody would blame you—"

"Somebody else killed her, Sammy."

"You mean somebody else from our show?" he asked. "Come on, Alexis."

"You said yourself she was a bitch. You even said you're not sorry she's dead. If the police hear you say that—"

"The police have already talked to me."

"Why? I didn't see you that day—"

"I was in the building. They're questioning everyone who was around that day, not just on the set," he explained. "But even they think you did it, Alex. If I were you, I'd get a lawyer."

"B-but I didn't do it." I got up quickly to leave, making the table rock.

"I forgot to get a drink," he said. "Are you gonna finish your coffee?"

I still had some scenes to tape and I'm a professional. Even though they were with Amanda, Sammy directing—two people who told me they thought I'd killed Marcy—I went ahead and did them. The show must go on, right?

When we were done I went directly to my dressing room, changed my clothes and left the building. It wasn't until I had dodged all the paparazzi—apparently they had discovered my not-so-secret exit—and got behind the wheel of my car that I had time to think.

If the police thought I'd killed Marcy, and my coworkers did, too, I was in more trouble than I'd realized. I thought—or hoped—I was just another suspect. I hadn't wanted to believe Paul when he said I would be suspect number one, but now . . .

I wasn't going to sit still for this. Bitch that she was, there must have been plenty of people who wanted to kill Marcy. All I had to do was find one of them. The right one.

# Chapter 15

Paul was supposed to come over that night, but I begged off. I was feeling confused and still wasn't ready to put my faith completely in a man. Besides, I was mad enough to want to do this myself. Maybe foolish enough, too, but there it was. All I had to do was figure out how to conduct my investigation. I had called earlier in the day to check on Sarah. My mother said her fever was down and, in a tutu and sparkle shoes, she was tearing up the house, pretending she was a chick superhero. Girls will be girls. We all had dinner together, and later Sarah diligently put sparkle pink nail polish on both her toes and her stuffed Bunny Bear's toes. I asked my mother to stay for some tea and collusion.

"Alex, what are you doing?" she asked, when I explained the situation to her. "Just let the police handle it."

"Mom," I said, "the police think I did it. Don't you understand?"

"But that one detective said he didn't believe you were guilty."

"He's not the lead detective on the case," I said.

"And besides that, I think he's a little bit of a whacko. He kept trying to call me Tiffany."

"Oh my," she said. "You've told me about people like that, who can't tell the difference between what's real and what's soap opera. And this is the detective who is actually on your side?"

"Tiffany's side, is more like it."

"Well then, what about Paul?"

"What about him?"

"Why not ask him for help?" she said. "Isn't this what he does?"

"Mom. I like Paul, but I just don't want to depend on him so much. It's too soon. And I feel like I'm not being fair to him."

"Alex . . ."

"What?"

"Paul *wants* you to depend on him."

"I'm not ready, Mom. We're doing just fine—you and Sarah and I are good on our own. I don't want her to get too attached. It's complicated. . . ."

"But you need him—"

"I don't need him! I can do this," I said. "I've watched so much court TV and cold-case shows I feel like I'm an expert. It's as if I've taken a course in it."

Okay, I know that sounded naive, but that's how I felt.

"How can you possibly know what to do next?"

"There are so many suspects," I said. "All I have to do is find the one who had the most to gain from Marcy's death."

"And how will you do that?"

"By talking to them."

"And if they won't talk to you?"

"I'll have to think of something else," I said. "Interview their neighbors, their families or best friends."

"How would you like it if someone did the same thing to you?" she asked.

"They are, Mother," I said. "They're called the police."

"At least talk to a lawyer," she said. "Your cousin Jennifer's husband is a lawyer—"

"He's a tax attorney, Mom. Look, I just need your help with Sarah so that I'm free to move around until this is over."

"What about work?"

"We're almost caught up," I said. "I have two scenes tomorrow, then a day off and then the weekend."

"All right," she said, "I'll help you, but on one condition."

"What is it?"

"By the beginning of next week, if you haven't managed to clear yourself of suspicion, you'll get help. I don't care if it's Paul, or a lawyer, or whoever, but you'll get some help."

I smiled at my mother and said, "It's a deal."

"There's my girl," she said, reaching across the table and patting my hand.

And unexpectedly I suddenly felt like a little girl again. I grabbed my mother's hand and held it.

"Mom, why is it so easy for people I work with to think I could do this?" *Mom, why won't the other kids play with me?* No wonder I related to Sarah's pre-K issues.

She put her other hand over mine and said, "Honey, sometimes people just naturally rush to judgment without thinking. It gives them comfort and makes them feel safe to put people and things in slots, whether they're the right ones or not. It's just easier for them to think it's you."

"Thanks, Mom," I said, squeezing her hand. "You always say the right thing. Well, almost always." She made a face at me and I made one back, and we laughed. Chicks rule.

That night, after my mother left and I finally got Sarah to bed, I turned on my laptop and checked my e-mails. Sure enough, there were two from Will. I opened the first and it was a long note.

*Alexis,*

*I did a background check on Marcy Blanchard and found that she married a man named Henry Roswell twenty years ago, in New York. They had a daughter two years later. Then, when they got divorced two years ago, the husband got custody of the daughter. They all still live in California. The husband is in Malibu. His address and some personal history are attached. I also have some personal stuff about the daughter, which I'll send in a second e-mail. I hope all of this helps.*

*Your friend,*
*Will*

The "your friend" at the end endeared the kid even more to me.

I managed to open the attached file without too much trouble. Sure enough, Henry Roswell's Malibu address was there, as well as some background on him. I fired up my printer and printed out the three pages.

Then I opened the second e-mail. The daughter's name was Julia Roswell. She was seventeen and, apparently, wanted to be an actress. There were some stills online, and Will had copied them for me. I wondered if Marcy had been planning on doing anything to help her daughter break into the business.

I printed out the file on the daughter. Since my printer didn't do color, the photos came out black-and-white, but I knew from the ones on the screen that she was a blonde, and very pretty. She looked a little bit like her mother, who hadn't exactly been ugly. There were no photos of her father in the e-mail, but I imagined he was handsome and had passed those genes along to the girl.

I took the printed pages and a cup of tea with me to my bedroom. I put them on the night table, then got myself ready for bed.

Even as I slid between the sheets I could feel my eyes starting to close. I tried to drink the tea and read the pages, but damned if I didn't drift off to sleep without finishing either of them.

# Chapter 16

The next day, as I told my mother, I had two scenes with Sammy directing. I decided to put his words behind me and get on with the job so I could start being what I've always wanted to be—an amateur detective. I stuffed the pages Will had sent me into my bag, hoping to read them later.

I decided to have my makeup done that morning by Linda; that way I'd have her cornered.

"I don't get to work on you very much, Alex," she commented.

"I'm lazy today, Linda. Besides, I'm supposed to look a little haggard—you know, dark circles under my eyes—and I can't quite muster up the courage to do that to myself."

"Great," she said, "I have to make you look less than beautiful. I get all the hard jobs."

"You're sweet," I said. "So, what have you heard about me killing Marcy?"

She almost poked me in the eye with a mascara brush.

"Alex!"

"Oh, don't play coy with me, Linda. I've been

hearing all the rumors." I'd already decided that my best course of action would be a straightforward one. Best offense, and all that.

"First, I think it's horrible that she was killed," Linda said. "Second, I don't believe for a minute that you did it."

"Well, thank you very much for that vote of confidence," I said. "And third?" Isn't there always a third?

"Third . . . I'm not sad that she's dead, and I guess that makes me a horrible person."

"If you are, then you're a member of a big club," I said. "I guess no one liked poor Marcy."

"That's because poor Marcy was a goddamned bitch," Linda said.

So far I'd heard her called a bitch, and a "royal," "true" and "goddamned" bitch. Everybody seemed to share the same basic opinion of her.

"Wow!" I said. "That's pretty harsh, coming from someone who really didn't have to work with her."

"Maybe not," she said, "but I did the makeup for a lot of people who worked with her, and let me tell you, plenty of them . . ."

My heart started to race.

"Plenty of them . . . what? Come on, Linda, don't cop out on me now."

"Well . . . I was going to say there are a lot of people who wanted her—who wouldn't have minded if she got herself—"

"Are you trying to say there are a lot of people with a motive to kill her?"

Linda looked at me in the mirror. "If you want to believe rumors."

*    *    *

Linda turned out to be Rumor Central. It was like reading a gossip column.

What studly soap actor was in danger of losing his job if he didn't agree to have a little fling with the head writer on the side?

What veteran actress—not me—had been reduced to running personal errands for a certain head writer in order to keep her part viable?

What aging soap actor had been driven by self-doubt—fueled by Marcy's treatment of him—to hire a life coach?

And what young staff writer had been forced to allow his own work to be presented as that of the head writer, who had run into a little case of writer's block?

Four likely suspects—in my eyes, anyway—and yet all of them had confided in Linda that they didn't "care" if I'd killed Marcy. And if they didn't care if I did it, did that necessarily mean they didn't?

And why would they air their grievances to Linda, who was so notorious for passing on rumors?

"Have you told the police any of this?"

"It's all gossip," Linda said carefully. "I'll tell you, I'll tell George, I'll tell some other people connected to the show, but why would I tell the cops? I don't want to cast suspicion on anybody."

"Because it could take some of the heat off me," I told her.

"Then why don't you tell them yourself?"

"Coming from me, it would just sound like I was trying to cover my own ass."

"Alexis," she said, tossing me a surprised look in

the mirror, "you want me to throw some other people to the cops so they'll stop looking at you?"

I hesitated, then said in frustration, "Noooo! That would just make me a horrible person, too, wouldn't it?"

I looked in the mirror and saw the dark circles Linda had put under my eyes.

"How is it?" she asked.

"Too damned good," I said. "Looks like me after a particularly bad night with Sarah."

"Well, then I guess my work here is done!" she replied.

# Chapter 17

I got through my two scenes and went to my dressing room. I had the distinct feeling that everyone on the show thought I was a killer. I could feel their eyes following every move I made. Despite the words of wisdom from my mother the night before, it was still very disconcerting to think that people I'd known for a long time—some of whom I thought of as friends—could even imagine I'd hurt Marcy. And to add to the frustration, some of them—most of them?—had obviously expressed their opinions to the police.

There were still several members of the cast I needed to talk to. But with the word going out—I knew Linda *wouldn't* be able to keep her mouth shut—that I was snooping around, I decided not to approach them at the studio. I knew where everybody lived, so I was going to conduct my interviews at their homes.

The same went for the ex-husband Marcy seemed to be trying to hide from me—Henry Roswell. I dressed in my street clothes—back to the comfort of my jeans and sweatshirt—and dug out the pages Will had sent me. I double-checked the Roswell address and saw that I'd be able to kill two birds with one stone. He lived right near one of the actors on the show, Andy McIntyre.

I read the background. Roswell was an investment banker, apparently good enough to eventually go out on his own, which was what he'd done when he moved to California with Marcy and their daughter. According to the info from Will, it was Roswell who had filed for divorce, citing the old standby "irreconcilable differences." Marcy had countersued with "alienation of affection," and "mental cruelty," but that obviously did not fly with the judge, who gave Roswell custody. A closer look at the dates told me that Marcy and her family had moved to California three years ago, and divorced just a year later.

There was more to read, but I needed to get moving if I wanted to squeeze some interviews in that day and still get home in time to have dinner with Sarah.

I began with Roman Stroud. He was one of the younger studs on the show—the stud who apparently had been forced to sleep with Marcy in order to keep his job. He started out playing a stable boy on the Benedict family estate. It must get pretty hot in those horse stalls, because Roman was sweaty and shirtless just about every day. Alas, he got Tiffany's younger half sister, Cicely, pregnant (on the show, remember) and in true soap opera fashion worked his way up from the tack room to the boardroom.

Roman's character, Tyler Sullivan, went from shoveling horse poop to becoming a high-powered executive in the land development empire in record time, but that hadn't stopped him from taking his shirt off.

His executive offices apparently had a shower and a steam room. Lots of opportunities for shirtlessness. We had had a few scenes together, mostly me screaming at him to get away from my sister, but I really hadn't gotten to know him very well. I found out he lived in Venice Beach, not far from where I lived, but in a funky apartment complex, inhabited by a lot of young twentysomethings like himself.

"He's not home," some very tan beach bunny said as she passed by me as I was knocking on Roman's door. "He's at the beach, working out in the pit," she added as she shifted her laundry to her other hip. "Aren't you that lady on Romy's show? My mom watches you every day."

"Thank your mom for me." I wondered if she'd heard of skin cancer.

I headed out to find Roman. Apparently he was honing his "skills" at Muscle Beach, just a short walking distance from where he lived. Muscle Beach was an outdoor workout area where bodybuilders went to see and be seen. I rounded the corner and sure enough, there was Roman, in all his sweaty glory. He was wearing a tight spandex number that left little to the imagination. No wonder the writers wanted to keep him in a towel.

"Alex, what are you doing here?" he asked, dropping a huge barbell on the mat.

"Looking for you," I said.

"Slumming?"

I was taken aback.

"Why would you say that?"

"You don't talk to me very much when we're on the

set," he said. "Makes me wonder why you would show up here. I mean, I'm not really in your circle of friends." He moved over to the heavy bag and started to punch it softly.

"Roman, as far as I know I don't really have enough friends at work to make a circle. I'm sorry. I had no idea you felt slighted. I'm kind of curious though. I mean, why are you so defensive?"

Now he was taken aback. I really had to work on my bedside manner.

"Why would I be defensive? You're the one everyone thinks killed Marcy." He started punching the heavy bag a little harder.

Now that pissed me off.

"That's exactly why I'm here. I didn't kill her. And I was wondering if you had heard of anyone else who might have a motive, you know, some hidden agenda involving Marcy?" I looked at him pointedly.

Now he got really uncomfortable. He stopped punching and just looked at me.

"You heard, huh?"

"Heard what?"

"Come on," he said, "you heard about me and Marcy, and you're gonna tell the cops! To get the focus off you!"

I decided to soften my approach.

"Roman," I said, "I'm not going to tell the cops anything. Let them find out their own information. I just—I'd like to know some things for my own benefit."

It sounded stupid even to me, but he seemed to buy it.

"Well, you must've heard the rumor that I—that

Marcy and I had a . . . thing." He resumed punching in a steady, rhythmic motion. Some of his sweat flung off and hit me in the face.

"I didn't hear it was a thing, exactly." I grimaced and brushed it off.

"You're right. It wasn't a thing," he said. "It was just sex. She told me if I wanted to get a decent story line, wanted to show off more than my chest, I had to sleep with her."

"She was that blatant about it?"

"Yes," he said. He punched harder.

"So . . ."

"So we did it a couple of times—in her office, in her car—and that was it."

In her car? Marcy, you cougar.

"What do you mean, that was it?"

"She lost interest."

"Come on," I said. "She's a lonely woman and she's got one of the young studs of the soap world in her bed . . . and she lost interest?"

"It wasn't about sex for her," he said. "I figured that out later. It was just about power." His punching was starting to make me nervous. Clearly, Roman had some anger issues. I wondered if they were big enough to make him kill.

"I guess you noticed that I still pretty much just walk around in a towel."

"So she didn't keep her word?"

"Nope." He grunted and hit the heavy bag so hard it flew off its chain. "Bitch!"

I backed away a little, "Bet that made you mad."

"Of course it did," he said, picking up a towel and

wiping off his brow. Then he backtracked when he realized how he must have sounded. "But not mad enough to kill her. I could never do that."

He swallowed hard and sat down on a bench. Was he, oh my God he was, he was crying. He wiped the snot from his nose.

"No, really, Alex—you're not gonna tell the cops, are you?"

From what I'd seen he was definitely not that good an actor. He was really scared. He had displaced anger and a cocky attitude, but unfortunately, he wasn't a killer.

"Roman," I said, "you should go and tell them yourself. It'd be better coming from you."

"I'll—I'll think it over. Maybe you're right," he said, looking me up and down. "Thanks, Alex."

"Sure."

He quickly collected himself and stood up. He moved in so close to me I could see every ripple of his very well-developed chest.

"Look," he said, "I'm sorry about before. You're not at all how I thought you were. You're not a—"

I was afraid he was going to say diva, so I said, "Bitch?"

"You're totally cool. And you're still hot. I mean considering you're pretty old. Maybe we should get together sometime after work, have a drink?"

Was he kidding? What an asshole!

"Oh, I can't. I'm seeing someone . . . uh, but, thanks."

"Sure, let me know if something changes."

He winked at me as he went back to his workout.

Hollywood.

# Chapter 18

I decided to try Andy next. I thought I could get him and Henry Roswell in, and then pick up Sarah. Then maybe do somebody else later in the day. I was glad that my scenes had been scheduled so early.

Andy McIntyre had started on the show about the same time I had. He played the role of police sergeant Hank Miller, the elder son of the broke but decent couple who had been cruelly taken advantage of by the Benedicts. In fact, Andy and I had played young lovers when we started on the show. You know, girl from rich, mean family falls in love with guy from poor, nice family. We have been involved in the same story lines off and on for years, and although we have great sexual chemistry on-screen, offscreen he's always been like a big brother to me. I have a lot of affection for him. Basically, we grew up together on TV and we'd been in the trenches.

In spite of being well into his forties, Andy looked great. He had dirty blond hair that fell kind of rakishly over his brow, and a slightly crooked smile that still made lots of women weak at the knees. He kept himself in shape and had maybe a little nip and tuck done

over the years. Not enough so that he looked pulled,
but just enough so that he looked "fresh." Unfortunately, he recently decided he hadn't accomplished
as much as he would have liked to in his life. He was
unmarried, no kids, bored with his job, trying to move
into directing, but just couldn't get self-motivated. He
had slowly acquired an entourage of sorts, over the
years. This consisted of a trainer, an assistant, fan
mail–answerer person, dog walker, feng shui expert
and God only knows what else. When Marcy came on
the scene, she did nothing but run him and his character down. I guess he decided that he needed additional
help with getting himself motivated. So he hired what
is called a "life coach." This is a phenomenon born
sometime in the nineties, I believe. I guess these people coach people in the game of life. Redundant, but
I'm still trying to figure out the concept.

Andy couldn't make a move without consulting
Murray. Murray the Life Coach. I know, misnomer.
Murray, I believe, used to sell insurance or something
until he discovered he had a certain "gift." I still don't
know what that gift is, but I do know it must be good
because he charges a lot of money. Andy is pretty
much paralyzed without the help of his coach. He's
constantly on his cell, asking for advice on everything
from what to have for lunch to should he sign a contract or not. During a particularly low point in Andy's
life, I guess Murray moved in and came to work with
him every day. He'd sit just off the set while Andy was
taping. Andy would run to him and ask how to play
the scenes in between takes. Now remember, this idiot
is a life coach, not an acting coach. Poor Andy's per-

formances became really odd, which did not endear him to the rest of the cast, the directors or to Marcy. He'd laugh and cry at inappropriate times, during scenes that just didn't garner those emotions. I also had heard that Murray was taking Andy to the cleaners, I mean big bucks, life savings cleaners. Usually I would stay out of such personal relationships, but I liked Andy, so I took him aside one day and had a good heart-to-heart. I asked him if he thought it was really necessary to keep Murray around, and maybe he just needed a good therapist or a nice, long vacation. He must have told Murray about my concerns, because I received a hateful letter from Mr. Coach, accusing me of trying to undermine Andy's career and "life goals"; he promised to make my life a living hell if I didn't butt out. Jeez! No good deed!

Andy lived in Malibu, near Paradise Cove where you could find anything from a million-dollar mobile home on the beach to a ten- to twenty-million-dollar colonial on the cliffs above. Andy's home was not quite in that class, so his neighbors were not quite Barbra Streisand and Julia Roberts.

I was hoping to be able to talk to Andy without Murray the Life Coach around, but that wasn't to be the case, because guess who opened the door when I rang the bell?

"Well, Ms. Peterson," Murray said. "What brings you here?" His yellow jogging suit was blinding, as well as incongruous. His swollen, distended belly was all the proof anyone needed that Murray did not exercise. The scent of patchouli wafted out the door, either from somewhere in the house, or from Murray himself.

"I'd like to talk to Andy, please, Murray."

I had to call him by his first name, because I still didn't know his last—unless it actually was "Life Coach."

"And what is this about?" he asked. "Not going to try and get me canned again, are you, hmm?" He touched his hand to his blow-dried do. The blow-drying was an attempt at poofing it up so that it might look thicker. Instead, I was able to see right through it to his shiny scalp.

"No, nothing like that, Murray," I said. "I learned my lesson last time. Your relationship with Andy is your business and his, not mine."

"Hmph," he said, probably because he was disappointed that he wouldn't be able to get into a fight with me. "Well, all right. Come in. He's out by the pool, going over his script for tomorrow. We were running lines together."

He led me through the house and out some glass doors to the pool area. Andy was sitting on a lounge chair with a drink next to him on a white metal table. He was wearing a robe that was open, revealing his swimming trunks and a physique he still worked hard to maintain.

"Don't say anything to interrupt the flow of his aura," Murray warned me. "He's very precariously perched at the moment."

I wanted to ask him where, but kept quiet.

"Andrew, you have a visitor," Murray announced, as we approached.

Andy lowered his script, saw me and couldn't hide the first flash that came across his face. I thought, not you, too, Andy.

"Alexis," he said, smiling broadly. He was a good actor, looked genuinely glad to see me, and on any other day I would have bought it. I was going to tell him to cut the act, but Murray was still there.

"What brings you here?" Andy asked.

"I just need a few minutes of your time, Andy," I said.

"No problem," he said, setting the script down on the table. "I always have time for you, you know that. Have a seat."

I sat across the table from him in a white chair that had come as part of the table set.

"What's on your mind?"

I didn't want to tell him what was on my mind while Murray was standing there, watching me.

"Um, is that coffee? I could use one."

"Oh, of course," Andy said. "I'm a terrible host. Murray, would you get Alexis some coffee? The Special Blend Number Five." He looked at me. "You'll love this. Murray has to go all the way across town to get this, but it's worth it."

"Um—," Murray started, but Andy shooed him away. "And bring me a fresh one."

As Murray left, Andy said, "He's like a mother hen sometimes."

"Andy, I have to say what I came to say before Murray gets back."

"Now, Alex, you're not going to ask me again to fire him, are you?"

"No," I said. "That's your business. I need to talk to you about Marcy's murder."

"Oh," he said, his face falling, "that."

"I know what everybody thinks, Andy, but I didn't do it," I said.

"I never thought—"

"Oh, sure you did. Everybody does. I can feel it when they look at me, and a couple of people have even told me so."

"Well," Andy said, "you did have that big screaming match with her . . . and after everything else you've been through, maybe she just pushed you too far."

"I am so sick of hearing that! Randy took my money and left our child. Yeah, it sucks! But I'm dealing! Things go wrong in life. It doesn't make a person a murderer, for God's sake! You *know* me! After all the time we've worked together I would think you, of all people, would know who I am and defend me."

I expected him to get angry, but instead he reached out, took my hand and said, "You're right. I've been a horrible friend to you. What can I do to redeem myself?"

I was taken aback for a moment, then felt a rush of affection for him. I squeezed his hand, and then we let go, sat back and started really talking.

# Chapter 19

"Since I didn't kill her, it's obvious somebody else did."

"I'm with you so far."

"Just hear me out before you say anything else," I said. He opened his mouth, but then closed it again and assumed a listening pose, chin and eyebrows up. For the moment I was assuming Andy didn't have his own motive for killing Marcy.

"There are a few people on the show who have had their issues with Marcy. I want your feedback on whether or not you think they hated her enough to kill her."

"Oh," he said, "oh, this is—you're investigating this yourself, aren't you? You must be so excited. You've always wanted to do this!"

At least he knew me that well. He was right; I had always wanted to do this, but not when my own freedom, or life, was on the line.

I pitched him some names—like Amanda, Roman and Dave Ballwin, the young writer whose work Marcy had been claiming as her own.

"I talked to Roman this morning," I said.

"I heard that story," Andy said. "Some people still try to sleep their way to the top."

"Well, I don't think Marcy was the top, but she did make him sleep with her a few times, and then dumped him. She never followed through by writing for him."

"That must have made him mad."

"I don't think he did it, Andy," I said. "After talking to him—he's cocky, yes, but basically just an overcompensating, insecure kid. It's not in him."

"Well, it's not in Amanda, either," Andy said, "and Dave, he's just trying to work his way up the ladder. He'll get credit, eventually. So in my opinion, it's neither of them."

I knew that, of course. Andy and I have been around the block, so he wasn't telling me anything I didn't know—just stuff I had to be reminded about, right now.

And then there is Lisa Daley. She's been with the show since its inception in the seventies. She's an attractive woman in her fifties. Her big problem in life is that she's still trying to play twenty-nine. This is where it can get ugly. And messy. Literally messy. She's had a decent amount of work done on her face, but nothing too extraordinary. It's just that now the fountain of youth comes in a syringe. Let me introduce you to the miracle twins: Botox and Restilane. Since they are now on the market, people can pretty much inject themselves up the wazoo. For all I know they inject there, too. Now, mind you, I'm all for maintenance. I know it's not always fun seeing yourself rotting away. But unlike most of the world, actors and actresses on soaps can see it on a daily basis. In color. On high-definition television. On a monstrous sixty-inch screen. It sucks! But you must practice self-control when it comes to the "injectables." Or you can turn out like Lisa. She has lost all sense of discretion and has so much stuff injected into her mouth she looks like one of the fishies in *Finding Nemo*. I saw her with a cup of coffee once and as she went to take a sip, she had no more feeling in her lips. The hot liquid just came pouring out of the cup onto her immoveable mouth and dripped all over her wardrobe. She wasn't even aware it had happened until I screamed for her to "step away from the cup." Her forehead has been injected to the point where she has absolutely no expression. Well, only one. No matter what she has to play, she looks the same, whether it is being sad, mad, glad. The same. Her face is utterly motionless. Her eyes express the various feelings needed. She looks like a trapped animal, eyes darting to and fro, up and down, trying to communicate inside a prison of Botox. She's very insecure and has a bad habit of referring to any pretty, new actress on the show as "What's her name." I guess it's a power play, her silly way of making that person feel unimportant. It's always seemed pretty weak to me.

Well, Lisa is the diva Linda said has been reduced to running Marcy's personal errands in order to keep her position on the show.

"It's been killing Lisa to pick up Marcy's laundry," Andy said. "Maybe Lisa decided to . . ."

"I'll have to talk to her, of course," I said. "Did you know Marcy had a husband? Well, an ex-husband."

"No, I didn't know that," he said.

"I guess she's been hiding it from us, or she'd just been denying it to herself. I'm going to talk to him as soon as I leave here. He lives nearby."

"He does? What's his name?"

"Henry Roswell."

"I know him." His eyes widened. "He lives right down the beach. It's a big glass house with a deck on the sand. He's got a pool, too. Very modern. You can walk there from here."

"How well do you know him?"

"Just to wave to on the beach. He's got a lovely daughter who—oh. No! Can that be Marcy's daughter?"

"Unless he's got another one."

"Jesus," Andy said. "Wow. Why would somebody deny a sweet kid like that?"

"Sweet?"

"She comes over here once in a while—you know, off the beach. I think she wants to be an actress. Jeez, you'd think her mother would have helped her out."

"Yeah, you'd think. Andy, do you have any more ideas about who'd want to kill Marcy?"

"Jesus, Alex," he said, "I would think pretty much anybody who knew her."

"Then why's everybody trying so hard to pin it on me?" I asked.

"Sorry," Murray said, coming back onto the scene. "I had to make it fresh—what happened?"

"What do you mean?" Andy asked.

"Your aura, it's changed." He glared at me. "What did you say to him?"

"You tell him, Andy," I said, standing up. "Thanks for your time."

"Don't you want to walk down the beach?" Andy asked.

I almost said no, I'd take my car, but then a walk on the beach sounded good. I hadn't done it in a while. "You know, I think I will."

"Okay, Alex," Andy said. "See you at the studio."

"Thanks for the coffee," I said as I passed Murray.

On my way to the beach I heard him saying to Andy, "Now relax, your aura is in flux. . . ."

# Chapter 20

When I got down to the sand I took off my shoes so I could walk barefoot. I loved the way the sand felt between my toes, and it seemed like it had been a really long time since I'd just gone for a stroll. The sun on my face was another luxury I hadn't enjoyed for a while. Along with the sound of the waves all of that suddenly made me want to take my surfboard out of dry dock. My cell started blaring and I saw that it was Connie, again. Not today, Con, sorry, and I pushed END.

I stopped at the flight of concrete steps that led up to the Roswell house, brushed off my feet and put my shoes back on. I took the steps up and found myself at the pool in back of the house. I wondered if I should work my way around to the front to ring the bell or knock on the back door. I didn't have to wonder long, though, as there was a young girl in a blue bikini sunning by the pool. She was wearing sunglasses and lying on a chaise longue.

"Hello," I called out.

She removed the glasses immediately and sat up. I noticed she had a swimmer's body—wide shoulders, small breasts. Once she removed the glasses I recognized her from the photos I'd seen online.

"You must be Julia."

She stared at me, blinking. I thought it was the sun, but then she said, "Omigod, you're Alexis Peterson."

"That's right."

She gaped at me for a few seconds more, then seemed to suddenly recall she was a teenager. She hurriedly put the glasses back on.

"What are you doin' here?" she asked.

"Well . . ." Suddenly, my mouth went dry. I assumed the police had notified Roswell about Marcy's death. And certainly it had been on the news. Julia must've been aware that her mother was dead, but what should I say?

"Are you lookin' for my dad?"

"Yes, I am."

"He's inside. I'll go get him."

She stood up, shook out her tawny hair and then walked to the house as if she were on a runway, or auditioning for me. But I remembered the look on her face when she recognized me. As an aspiring actress, she'd been impressed. That was good for my ego. And she was certainly also well aware of the fact that I worked on her mother's show.

She had gone through sliding glass doors, closing them behind her, and now she returned with a tall, very handsome man in tow. Henry Roswell obviously worked out. He was built along the lines of a tennis player. I knew he was in his mid-forties, but he moved like a much younger man. Only the gray at his temples gave him away, and I liked that he wasn't vain enough to color it.

"Ms. Peterson?" he asked in a deep-timbre voice.

If I'd ever seen him and Marcy together as husband and wife I would have thought, Marcy girl, you did good. He was kind of a dreamboat.

"Mr. Roswell?" I asked. "I worked with Marcy on—"

"I know who you are, Ms. Peterson." When he reached me he put his hand out. "It's a pleasure to meet you. What can I do for you?"

"Well . . ." I hesitated, and looked at Julia.

"Julia knows about her mother, Ms. Peterson," he said. "You can speak in front of my daughter."

"All right—," I said.

But before I could go any further he asked, "Can I get you something to drink? I'm being a bad host."

"No, I'm fine, thanks."

"Then let's sit," he invited.

There were chairs around the pool, as well as a couple of chaise longues, but no table. He pulled two chairs over so we could sit, and Julia sat back down on her longue.

"I can only assume your visit has something to do with Marcy's murder."

Julia made a slight noise and her father reached over to touch her knee.

"Yes, it does," I said, and my mouth went dry again. What questions should I ask? What ever made me think I could conduct an interview, or even a full-fledged investigation? Once again I found myself wishing I was on a surfboard out in the Pacific.

"I really don't know what I can tell you," Roswell said. "I hadn't seen Marcy since the divorce."

"Julia?" I asked. "Had you seen your mother recently?"

Julia wet her lips and looked at her father.

"Go ahead, honey. You can answer her question."

Julia looked as if she wanted to get up and run. I had the feeling she had something to say but didn't want her father to hear.

"Why should I?" she asked.

"Julia—"

"No," Julia said, standing up. "We've already talked to the police. Why should we answer her questions? Who is she, anyway?"

She turned and stormed into the house.

"I'm sorry," he said. "She's distraught. I can tell you that Julia hasn't seen her mother in months. The truth is Marcy was simply denying us this past year, refusing to admit we even existed. She thought we were both mistakes in her life."

"I can't understand a mother denying her child," I said, thinking of how much I loved Sarah.

"The truth is," he said, "we never should have gotten married, and probably never should have had a child. I don't know how we stayed together for so long—we were such different people. But . . . I hear so many couples say that. But I love Julia dearly. If there was some way I could go back and not marry Marcy, yet still have Julia . . ."

"I know exactly what you mean."

"You have a child?"

"A daughter, and an ex."

"Then you do understand."

I did. All too well.

"I married Marcy on the rebound from some great love, if you can believe that." He dismissed Marcy's "great love" with a wave of his hand. "I can't believe it lasted as long as it did. I always paled by comparison."

I had known Marcy's great love, and there was no way I could see his memory eclipsing this man right in front of me. Marcy was such a fool.

"Ms. Peterson—"

"Alexis, please."

"Alexis," he said, "what is the purpose of your visit? Were you Marcy's friend?"

"Actually," I said, "Marcy and I didn't get along at all, Mr. Roswell."

"Henry, please."

"Henry . . . To tell you the truth I'm just . . . nosing around, trying to see what I can find out."

I thought he might grow angry at my confession, but he didn't. He was handsome and sensitive—too good to be true. I guess if he had a flaw it was probably his taste in women.

"I guess her murder hit pretty close to home for her coworkers, even if they didn't like her very much."

"Yes, it did."

He reached his hand out and placed it on mine. Was he being sincere or was he just another operator?

He squeezed and said, "I'm sure it's been upsetting. If I can do anything to help you—"

I pulled my hand away from his, trying not to do it too fast, and said, "I was just wondering if you knew anyone in her personal life who might have wanted to kill her."

He took his hand back and said, "I really don't know anything about her personal life. Oh, I see. You're hoping that the killer was not someone connected to the show. Well, I can see how you'd like that to be the case."

He had kind eyes, but I suddenly remembered what he did for a living. He dealt with high finance, bankers, investors—he was a salesman. Considering where he lived, he was apparently quite good. And then suddenly, instead of looking kind, he looked kind of crafty. I had the feeling I was being played.

"Well," I said, standing, "I won't take up any more of your time."

He stood, also.

"Would you like to go out through the house?"

"Yes, thank you. My car is in front."

As we walked through the house he asked me how I came to be on the beach and I told him that my friend Andy McIntyre lived a few houses down. He said he didn't know him.

His house was a huge modern, in a different class than Andy's, and he was quite proud of it. In fact, I think he walked me through it instead of around just to try to impress me. But he was too late; he'd already lost me outside.

He held the door open for me, took my hand and said, "It was a pleasure meeting you, Alexis."

"Thank you," I said, and left. He was handsome and charming, but he was way too smooth to suit me.

It was a long walk to the street and when I got there, Julia was waiting, her arms folded across her chest.

"I couldn't talk in front of my dad," she said.

"I understand, Julia."

"I went to see my mother last month," she said. "I told her I wanted to be an actress, and she threw me out.

"I don't know who killed her," she said. "Maybe you did, but I don't care. I'm not sorry she's dead. She made my dad miserable, and she wouldn't help me with my career. As a mother she really sucked."

"Where did you go to see her, Julia? At the studio?"

"I went to her house," Julia said. "My dad doesn't know, and I don't want him to."

"He won't find out from me."

She kept her arms folded tight and, except for the bikini, looked like a stubborn little girl.

"I mean it," she said. "If you did it, I don't care. I'm glad she's dead."

Before I could say anything else she turned and stormed off toward the house.

Walking back to my car I couldn't help but think, poor Marcy.

# Chapter 21

As it turned out, I didn't have time for any more interviews. I picked up Sarah, and she needed some mom time. I spent the rest of the day and evening with her—loving every minute—before she finally went to bed.

I make sure we always have together time when I get home. I don't know if she'd miss it if we didn't, but I certainly would.

After I had her tucked in and read to, I had some reading of my own to do. I went through all the material Will had e-mailed me. It was very stiff and formal info on Julia and her father, but I had learned more in the short time I'd spoken with them both. I also checked my cell's voice mail. Connie had called twelve times. In the last two days. I braced myself and called her back.

"Connie, before you start, I have to tell you that now is just not a good time for anything else on my plate, okay? Especially these silly jobs. I've got a job, at least for now, and—"

"Al! I know you're goin' through so much crap. I get it! But you have to think of your fuckin' career. You have to take advantage of all this fuckin' media attention, sweetie! Now, before you hang up, *CSI*—the good one—wants you on the show! Whaddya think of that? Is that some awesome shit, or what?"

Now that got my attention. I liked the show and I liked the subject matter . . . forensics, that is.

"What's the part? I'd even do a little part on that show. I'm sure it must be kind of juicy, right?"

"Well, now here's the thing. You'd be a corpse." I could sense Connie was gearing up for some tap dancing.

"There have to be flashbacks or something before she's a corpse, right?"

"Not exactly. You'd be in the morgue. It's one shot, but a very important one! They'd put a lot of that white makeup on you to make you look dead. It could be fun! There's a little dialogue. Al, wait—" Again, I hung up.

Thankfully, I had the next three days off from work, so my plan was to get my surfboard wet in the morning. I was hoping some time on the waves would clear my head and give me a clearer picture of what I had to do. If I wasn't able to see my next move clearly, it might be time to ask Paul for help. I was sure he'd like that a lot. He'd been waiting awhile for me to finally lean on him.

I went to sleep with that thought in mind and dreamed that when I finally asked Paul for help he refused. "Too late, babe," he said, in my dream. "That ship has sailed."

\*　　　\*　　　\*

When I woke the next morning I remembered the dream, but knew after a few minutes it would fade. That's the way it is with most dreams. Thankfully.

I may have had the day off from work as an actress, but I, thankfully, never had the day off as a mom. I made breakfast for Sarah, ate with her, laughed with her, kissed her and took her to pre-K. With a few hours to myself I went back home and got out my surfboard.

Yeah, it had been a while since I'd been in the water. I actually had to brush off a few cobwebs when I took my nine feet four off the racks in my garage. Now that's kind of depressing! Talk about needing a little "me" time. A nine feet four is a fairly big board, and I had to be careful not to whack anything (like my head) as I gently put my board on my car and strapped it down. I grabbed my shortie (wet suit) because the water hadn't been too cold lately, threw some wax in my bag and hopped in my car. The beach was just a block or two away. I could have walked, but let's not get carried away. I wanted to conserve my energy for the waves . . . right? I pulled up in the parking lot, hopped out and got my board down from the top of my car. Walking out to the beach I surveyed the water. The waves weren't too big and they had nice shape. It also wasn't too crowded out there, which was rare these days. It seemed that everybody and their mother, literally their mother, was surfing. There was a time, not too long ago, when I'd be the only "chick" out with all the boys. Which was kind of nice, because guys were very chivalrous in the water and likely to share a wave or two. Anyway, I threw my wet suit on, being careful not to get my hair trapped in the zipper, plopped my board down on the sand, grabbed my wax and knelt down to put a little on my board. Then I put a little extra on just to make sure I wouldn't slip off. I'd need all the help I could get. I was rusty.

Like I said, it had been a while since I'd paddled out, and I immediately felt it in my arms and back. It hurt, but it was a good kind of pain. When I got to a good spot, I sat up and waited for a wave. Being out there in the middle of the water was the best form of meditation. There's that word again. I need to meditate on why I feel I need to meditate.

I started thinking about everything that had happened over the past few days. It seemed to me the most idiotic thing about it was that anyone would think I could kill Marcy. I'd never thought of it that way before, but it kind of hurt my feelings. Okay, so maybe the cops thought I did it. That's what they're paid to do, suspect people. But everyone I worked with? Come on!

The thought of it brought me closer to tears than I'd been since it happened. What if I did get arrested for the murder? What would happen to Sarah? She'd already lost her father. The thought of my beautiful little girl without a father or mother . . . Suddenly, I was tasting salt. At first I thought it was the ocean, but then I realized tears were flowing. No sobs or anything, just tears mixing with salt water. I let them come. Tears of sadness, of anger, frustration . . . I let them all come out there on the water where no one could see me, just to get them out of my system.

When I was done having a good cry I slammed my hand down on the board, wiped tears and salt water from my face with the heels of my hands and tried to bring my thoughts back to the business at hand. Who killed Marcy? Didn't I have to do the same thing as the cops in order to clear myself? I had to suspect everyone I worked with of being a killer.

The onset of a wave interrupted my thoughts. When you're surfing it's a good idea to pay attention to what you're doing. I turned around to face the beach and started paddling. As the wave grew and took shape, I paddled faster and faster until I could feel I had the wave under me and behind, propelling me. I stood up, not as gracefully as I would have liked, but hey! For the first time in a long while I felt free as I worked the wave up and down. I kept going and going until the wave dissolved into the shore.

This was just what I needed. I felt exhilarated and empowered . . . as if I could do anything. And oh, how I would need this kind of confidence for what I needed to do next.


There were other coworkers to interview, but they didn't have the day off, like I did, and I didn't want to go to the studio.

Her ex had not been able to tell me anything about Marcy, presumably because he didn't know anything about her. Although they technically still lived in the same city, they had no contact with each other. I didn't know who exactly had abandoned whom. Maybe they'd abandoned each other. But Marcy had pretty much cut her daughter off. For a moment I wondered if a seventeen- or eighteen-year-old girl could kill her mother. Then I decided no, the girl I had talked to could not. The poor kid was angry, probably more hurt, but I didn't think she was a murderer. For one thing, she would have had to get on the lot, and to do that somebody would have had to leave her a pass. It didn't seem likely after turning her away—refusing to help her with her career—that Marcy would leave her a pass.

I wasted most of the morning after surfing. Well, maybe not wasted. I spent it thinking in a shower, and then over a cup of tea. Finally it was time to pick up Sarah. I'd left my mother alone, given her time to herself, because I knew I was going to ask her to stay with Sarah that afternoon.

"Where are you going?" she asked, while the three of us had lunch together in the big house.

"I'm going to talk to some people," I said.

"Suspects?" my mother asked.

"Yes, Mother, suspects."

I wondered what my mother was going to have to say to that after we'd already discussed my plan to conduct my own investigation. I didn't have very long to wait.

She looked at me with concern as I carried our lunch dishes to the sink and said, "Keep yourself safe, honey."

Little did I know. . . .

# Chapter 22

My plan was to take the kid car and go to Marcy's home. I knew where it was because she'd had a "let's get acquainted" cocktail party when she landed the job. It was there that I first realized she must still be holding a grudge, because she glared at me all night. I've never been there again—never been invited.

However, when I opened my front door, I found my way blocked by the press. I guess word had finally gotten out about my address. Cameras flashed in my face; questions were lobbed at me; I even saw a tape recorder or two. And then I saw Detective Jakes, bullying his way through, knocking people aside.

"Watch it, asshole!"

"Who the hell is this guy?" a short, fat man yelled.

"Come with me," Jakes said, putting his arm firmly around me.

He got us through the crowd without letting anyone touch me, which was impressive. He used his elbow and shoulders and got us to his car. After he placed me in the passenger seat he turned and shouted at everyone, "That's all for today. Clear out of here." Then he walked around and got behind the wheel.

"Good morning, Ms. Peterson."

"Maybe for you. Excuse me, Detective, I have to call my mother." I fished my cell phone out of my bag and quickly hit speed dial. "Mom, the press is all over the place. Just stay put with Sarah. Now that they know I've left, things should calm down. Just stay inside until you hear from me, okay? . . . I love you, too.

"Detective Jakes," I said, closing my phone, "How . . . nice. Thank you for saving me."

"I've had experience with press mobs before."

"Press mobs?"

"Press with a mob mentality," he said. "They'd trample you to get a story, even if it was only 'Soap Queen Trampled by Press.'"

Jakes laughed, showing very white teeth. He really was rather good-looking.

"Soap queen?"

"I thought you'd like that better than 'diva,'" he said.

"Actually, I don't like either. Um, how do you propose to get me to my car now?"

"There's no need. I'd like you to come with us, if you would."

"Where?"

"What is it they always say on TV?" he asked. "Downtown?"

"And why would I want to go downtown with you and your partner?"

"Just to answer a few more questions."

"Can't you ask them here?"

"Here? On the street with that crowd around us? Or inside, in front of your daughter?" He smiled what seemed like a very condescending smile. "No, I'm afraid this has to be . . . official."

"Am I under arrest?" I asked. My mouth was dry.

"Oh, no," he said, "no, nothing like that. You are, however, what we refer to as a 'person of interest' in this case."

"Not a suspect?"

"We could upgrade you to suspect," he offered. "Would you prefer that?"

"What I would prefer, Detective, is not to play games."

"Good," he said, "then why don't you come with us and just answer our questions?"

"Can I follow you in my own car?" I asked.

"I don't think you want to brave this mob again, do you?"

I turned my head and jumped. One of them had his face pressed against the window, and was shouting questions at me.

"Actually, I trust you to get me to my car safely."

He sighed, then opened his door and said, "Okay, let's do this . . . again."

They took me to an interview room in Parker Center, LA police headquarters, which actually was located in downtown LA. They asked me if I wanted coffee or tea; I took tea. I actually felt like having it. It was Davis who brought it to me, and I thought he gave it to me along with a reassuring look.

They each had a cup of coffee and we all sat down at a table, them on one side, me on the other.

"Ms. Peterson, we need to be a little more specific

with our questions than we were the other day," Jakes said. "Is that all right?"

"Excuse me but isn't this the part where you're supposed to ask me if I want a lawyer?" I interrupted.

Jakes paused and sighed.

"You're not under arrest, Ms. Peterson," he said. "Technically you're not even a suspect yet. We're just asking you to . . . help us out. Is that all right?"

I was tempted to ask what would happen if it wasn't all right, but instead said, "That's fine." After all, I had nothing to hide.

"You and the victim had a history, did you not?"

"Yes, we did. But I'm sure you've heard about this from others."

"We need to hear it from you, Alex. Do you mind if I call you Alex?"

"No, I don't mind."

"If I hear it from you, Alex," Jakes said, "it'll be the truth, won't it?"

"Yes," I said, "it will."

"Okay," Jakes said, "tell me the history between the two of you."

I did, as straightforwardly as possible. Both men listened and did not interrupt. I thought that Davis, as a soap opera fan, was probably enjoying it more than his partner.

"All right," Jakes said, "that explains your past. Now tell me about the shouting match the two of you had last week."

I had no reason to tell them anything but the truth. I told them how Marcy had been treating me since she took over the show, how I'd had enough the previous week and had gone to have it out with her.

"Tell me how your fingerprints got on the murder weapon," Jakes asked.

"It was last week, while we were yelling at each other. I picked it up. I was going to throw it, but I was afraid it would break, so I just sort of . . . tossed it in her direction and ran out."

Jakes looked at Davis. I didn't see anything pass between them, but something must have. Maybe they'd been partners longer than I originally thought. Davis got up and left the room.

"How did you pick it up?" Jakes asked.

"I grabbed it around . . . the legs, just above the base."

"Was that the way you would have grabbed it to hit her with it?"

"What? I don't know. I had no intention of hitting her with it."

"What if she had come at you?" he asked. "What if she'd tried to get it away from you?"

"Are you saying that I hit her with it and killed her during a struggle?"

"Like I said, Alex," he replied, "I'm just asking more specific questions than I did the other day."

"Yes," I said, "yes, you are."

# Chapter 23

The door opened and Detective Davis came walking back in. He was carrying the Emmy, which was encased in a plastic evidence bag. He set it upright on the table and went back to his chair.

"I never saw one of these up close until this case," Jakes said, pointing to the statuette. "Which is actually kind of odd, since I work in Hollywood. I've seen three Oscars, but never an Emmy." He turned around. "Hey Len, how many Oscars you seen?"

Davis held up two fingers.

"Any Emmys?"

"Nope."

Jakes looked at me.

"Maybe it's not so odd, then."

"Do you have a question for me, Detective?" I asked.

"Oh, yeah, I do," he said. "Sorry. This is the actual murder weapon."

"I assumed that when I found the body with it under the desk."

"Really? Why would you assume that?"

"It had blood on it," I said. "The blood hadn't coagulated yet. I figured she'd just been killed, probably while we were all watching the light fixture fall. Also, rigor hadn't started yet."

"Well, okay," Jakes said. "Maybe you do know a little bit about my business. My point, though, is still that your prints are on this."

"So?"

"Would you come around here and stand next to me, please?"

I was going to protest, but then decided just to do as he asked and get it over with.

"Now turn and face Detective Davis, please."

I did so. Davis looked bored, very unlike the soap fan I'd had coffee with three days ago—was it three days ago, already? No, two. And three since Marcy had been killed. It didn't seem possible that that much time had gone by.

"Alex?"

"Oh, yes, I'm sorry," I said. "I was . . . thinking of something."

"Am I boring you?"

I was tempted to say yes, but I just shook my head.

"Okay, let's say Len—Detective Davis—is Ms. Blanchard, and you've just had your, uh, screaming match. As you leave, you grab the Emmy and . . . what? Show me."

I stared at him.

"What do you want me to do?"

"Throw it."

"Where?"

"At Len—Detective Davis."

"It—it'll break."

"You didn't worry about that the other day," Jakes said.

"Yes, I did," I said. "That's why I didn't throw it, I just . . . sort of . . . tossed it."

"Okay," Jakes said, "Show us. Toss it."

I looked at the Emmy, residing in its plastic evidence bag.

"Just pick it up with the bag," Jakes said, "and toss it."

I still stared at it. I remembered how angry I was at Marcy, and how I wanted to throw the Emmy right at her, maybe take off her head. I didn't feel that now.

"I can't—"

"Throw it!" Jakes shouted at me, galvanizing me into action. I grabbed the Emmy right in the center and tossed it at Davis, who caught it easily.

"That's it?" Jakes asked. "That's how you threw it at Marcy?"

"I told you," I said, my voice rising, "I didn't throw it."

"You tossed it."

"That's right."

Jakes looked at Davis, who seemed to give him a look that said, "See?" I guess Davis was my—or Tiffany's—champion.

"Okay, Alex," Jakes said. "You can go."

"I can?"

"Of course," Jakes said. "We're done." He perched a hip on the table, looking very relaxed.

"Am I . . . a suspect?"

"Like I told you before," Jakes said, "everybody's a suspect."

"You haven't . . . um, crossed anybody off your list yet?"

"Oh, sure we have," Jakes said. "Quite a few people, in fact." Then he smiled and added, "But not you. Not yet. Don't leave town."

"Where would I go?"

"I don't know, really," Jakes said. "I just like saying that."

I looked over at Davis, who jerked his head toward the door. Was he telling me to get out while I could?

I got out.

And ran smack dab into a media frenzy.

"Did you do it, Alex? Did you kill Marcy? You hated her, right?" Flash, flash. I stopped myself from smacking one particularly annoying photographer who closely resembled a Chihuahua nipping at my heels. I jumped into my car and *really* got going.

# Chapter 24

I admit I was rattled during the ride home. For a few reasons. I almost rode up on the bumper of an SUV carrying several kids. I braked in time, thank God, and tried to concentrate the rest of the way home on both the road and my predicament—which raised many questions.

What had I proved or disproved for Detective Jakes by tossing the Emmy to Detective Davis the way I had? How much was Davis on my side—or my character, Tiffany's? Whom had Jakes eliminated as a suspect? And why had he made certain I knew I wasn't one of them?

They had released me just in time to pick Sarah up from her ballet lesson, to which my mother had driven her. I took her home, listening with half an ear to her stories about the day. I hated not giving my little girl my full attention, but what are you gonna do? I couldn't be all things all the time. Actress, mommy, detective . . . murder suspect, something had to suffer! My mind was a jumble of thoughts and very few ideas. I needed to clear my head, but this time instead of surfing I decided to take the Speedster out for a spin.

When we got home the press had cleared out. They must have all gone to Parker Center, thank God.

I took Sarah right to my mom's little house and since she knew I was still playing amateur detective, Momma took her without a word. (They loved each other so much I knew they'd have a ball together.) I really needed to get the Porsche out on the road.

I eased Marilyn out of the garage, and settled into her old leather seat. (No, I didn't name my car after Marilyn Monroe. The previous owner did and despite my valiant efforts, the name stuck.) It felt so good having the gearshift in my hand. I looked over the dashboard like a pilot about to take off and pulled out onto Washington Boulevard. I was itching to put her into fourth, but I had to restrain myself and settle for enjoying the sound of her engine. Marilyn wanted to break out, too, so we headed off to Ocean Boulevard, passing the old craftsman houses and the occasional homeless person. In a few minutes I was cruising down PCH. I decided to take her to Malibu even though this time of day would mean traffic. There is a stretch of PCH north of Zuma Beach that is less congested. Maybe you've heard of it? Some guy a year or two ago took a Ferrari out and raced it against a Mercedes. He ended up crashing his car, then running away. I would try to be more careful.

I started to relax as I purred past the multimillion-dollar beach houses. This part of California is as beautiful as any in the world. If you didn't know better, you would think you were somewhere on the Italian coast.

I took a deep breath and finally began to process my situation.

I couldn't even believe that I was seriously considered a murderer. It still boggled my mind. Ultimately, I was wondering what it meant. I mean how did I attract this situation into my life and why? Was I supposed to learn something from it? (I mean other than the fact my cast mates thought I could kill?) I was a firm believer in the "everything happens for a reason" mentality. I'd lived in LA long enough that some airy "fairiness" was bound to rub off. But if God or the universe or the "whatever" was trying to make a point, couldn't they just spit it out? Why be so vague? Take out a billboard for God's sake!

Before I knew it, traffic had cleared out and I had a stretch of PCH basically to myself. I smoothly moved the shift into fourth and let her rip. For about ten seconds. Not that long but long enough for me to get a taste of what Marilyn was built for. I pulled over to the side of the road and watched the sunset. Perspective. I had to have faith this would all work out and make sense eventually. Just keep putting one foot in front of the other.

I had my cell with me and suddenly decided to try to call Lisa Daley. She'd been with the show a long time, so I had her in my directory.

"Alex, hi," she said. "You caught me coming in the door. I just left the studio."

"Hello, Lisa."

"Let me put a few things down . . . there. How are you? It must be hell catching flack in the press over this Marcy business."

"I'm weathering the storm, Lisa," I said, wondering how to approach her. "I know the police are looking at some other people, so I'm not that worried."

"Other people?"

"You know, people connected with the show who might have had a grudge against Marcy."

"Well, they've spoken to me, of course, but I thought . . . um, I thought they were satisfied with what I told them. . . ."

"Lisa, I'm sure if you told them the truth—"

"I didn't," she said, suddenly. "I didn't tell them the truth. That's going to be bad for me, isn't it?"

I could see her in my mind's eye gnawing on a nail. She did that when she was nervous, or stressed. The directors hated it.

"Lisa, whatever you held back, I'm sure . . ."

"Sure what? Somebody else will tell them?"

"Well, it happened to me," I admitted. "I didn't tell them about my fight with Marcy, but they found out."

"Oh God," she said, "you know what she was doing to me, don't you? Treating me like a gopher . . . a . . . nobody?"

"I'd heard something about that."

"I hated that mean, conniving bitch, Alex," Lisa said, "but I didn't kill her. I could never do . . . what someone did to her. I could dream about it, but not do it, you know, with my own hands."

I could see what my problem was going to be with this amateur-detective gig. I was believing everyone.

"I'm sure you didn't, Lisa."

"What should I do?"

"Why don't you just wait for the police to ask you

about it," I said. "They might not feel that it's enough of a motive for murder."

"But I think it is, Alex."

"What?"

"I think if she was treating someone else like this, they might have killed her. Someone . . . stronger than I am."

"Just because you didn't kill her doesn't make you weak."

"Thank you, Alex. Listen, I—I have to go. . . . Thanks."

"Sure," I said. "Bye."

# Chapter 25

It was pretty close to dark when I drove Marilyn back onto PCH and headed south.

I was still more inside myself when I pulled the car into the garage and hit the button to close the door behind me, so I guess I could be forgiven—or taken to task?—for what happened next.

The lights went out.

Well, they didn't really go out. That's the way I've seen it put in books, and the movies. What actually happened was I opened the car door, stepped out and got hit on the head. Instant pain, then blackness, and the rest of it was a jumble. . . .

I felt somebody grab me under the arms, drag me. . . .

My eyes wouldn't focus. I saw a bulky figure, but couldn't make out the face. . . . If the person spoke to me I never heard a voice because there was a ringing in my ears. . . .

Then came a smell. I knew it well, and knew that it was bad, but I couldn't move. . . .

Coughing woke me up, and I wondered who was

choking up a lung, and then realized it was me. . . . Still couldn't move. . . .

I didn't see any white lights, but I either dreamed or hallucinated . . . I was surfing, all the time wondering why it smelled like I was driving. . . . The ocean didn't smell like that. . . . There was no salt, just . . . fumes. . . .

And then there was a crash, and a bright light, and once again someone was grabbing me beneath the arms, lifting me, taking me into that light. . . . Was this the way it happened? I'd heard the stories about bright lights and spirits who helped you cross over. . . .

Someone slapped my face, and suddenly I could move. I swiped at the hand as it slapped me again, and then I heard Paul saying, "Alex, Alex, can you hear me? Alex!"

"Damn it, Paul," I heard myself say, "stop slapping me!"

The paramedics came and strapped an oxygen mask over my face. I could see dark fumes drifting out from the open garage.

I tried to talk, but the mask was an impediment, so I tried to remove it.

"Leave that on, miss," a paramedic said.

As I continued to struggle to get the mask off, I saw my mother, and Paul, but not Sarah.

"Sarah," I said, into the mask.

Paul understood me.

"Sarah's fine," he said. "Don't worry. She's at your mom's with a policewoman."

"Police—," I said, looking around. Sure enough,

there were some uniformed police wandering around, peering into the garage. The door seemed to be hanging at an odd angle.

"Nice car," I heard one say.

"Messed up this garage door, though," another one replied.

I looked up at Paul and asked, "What happened?" Although it sounded like "Wha-hoppen?"

"When can we take that off her?" Paul asked the paramedic.

Before he could answer, someone else said, "How about now, so we can find out what the hell happened here?"

I craned my neck to see who was speaking and saw Detectives Jakes and Davis standing there.

"Who are you?" Paul demanded.

"Jakes," Jakes said, "and my partner, Davis. LA Homicide Desk. We had a talk with Ms. Peterson just this morning, and then heard this call come over the radio a few hours later." Jakes pointed and Davis walked over to the garage. "And you?"

"Paul Silas."

"Oh, you're the forensic boyfriend, right?"

"What did you talk to her about this morning?" Paul asked.

"Just some aspects of the Marcy Blanchard case," Jakes said. He looked at the paramedic. "Can we take that mask off now? For a few minutes?"

"Just a few," he said. "She inhaled a lot of that crap. She should go to the hospital."

"She will," my mom said. "I'll make sure of it."

"And you are . . . ," Jakes asked.

"Her mother."

"Nice to meet you," Jakes said, and dismissed her.

The paramedic took the mask off and I noticed that he looked like someone who wasn't old enough to even shave yet.

"How old are you?" was the first thing I said when the mask came off.

"I think she's all right," the kid said. "I'm thirty, ma'am, but I look young for my age."

"Excuse me," Jakes said, and the paramedic stepped aside.

I realized I was lying on a stretcher and, thankfully, he stepped between me and the sky. The sun wasn't high, but it was still pretty bright.

"Alex, can you tell me what happened?" Jakes asked.

"I—I don't know," I said. "I went for a drive, came back, pulled into the garage . . . the rest is a blur. . . ."

"I'm afraid you're gonna have to do better than that," he said.

"I can't . . . I don't even know . . ."

"Okay, that's enough," Paul said, stepping between me and Jakes. "She's disoriented and can't answer any questions."

"Well, she's gonna have to—," Jakes started, but Paul wasn't having any.

"She's going to the hospital to be checked over," Paul said. "If you want to talk to her, you'll have to wait for visiting hours."

Jakes and Paul were standing nose to nose, but suddenly I was no longer privy to their argument.

I heard the paramedic say, "She's going under. . . ."

# Chapter 26

"Suicide."

I woke up with a start, then looked around to see where I was. A hospital room, and I was in semidarkness. Over by the door I saw Paul talking with two nurses; he seemed to be scolding them.

I tried to speak but nothing came out. There was the most foul taste in my mouth I'd ever experienced. I lifted my arm and waved until one of the nurses saw me. She said something to Paul and her coworker; then they came over to the bed while the first nurse walked away.

"Hey, sweetheart," the nurse said. She was probably close to my age but looked about ten years older. "How you doin'?"

"W-water," I managed to rasp.

"I got it," Paul said. He poured some from a plastic pitcher into a plastic cup, then put in a straw and held it to my mouth. It was the best thing I'd ever tasted. I nodded and he took the cup away.

"Can I get anything else for you?" the nurse asked.

I shook my head and pointed to Paul.

"I'm sorry, sugar, but your husband is going to have to leave. Visiting hours are over—"

"He's not my husband! Just a minute," I said, "I want to talk to him . . . for a minute."

"I'm sure we can have five minutes, right, Nurse?" Paul asked.

A conspiratorial look passed between them and she said, "Well, all right, but just five. I'll be right down the hall. You have this little button here—"

"I've got it," I said. I'd been in the hospital once in real life and many times in the soap opera world. It seemed that whenever my contract was up for renegotiation Tiffany was put in a coma until the network and I could come to an agreement. If I agreed to their terms, Tiffany miraculously awoke; if not, then Tiffany sadly would pass on (supposedly). Not to mention Tiffany had fallen off a cliff or two, had been mugged once, miscarried twice and was involved in several fires and earthquakes. Tiff had had a rough life. My real life was quickly catching up to my alter ego's life, and that made me uncomfortable.

When we were alone I asked, "W-what happened?"

"I came over to see you and nobody answered the door. I thought about going around back to your mom's house, but decided to check the garage instead. I don't know why. When I got to the door I heard a motor running inside and realized fumes were coming from beneath it. I tried to open it, but it wouldn't budge. I tried the back door and it was locked. Finally, I just drove my truck into the garage door a few times until it buckled."

He loved that truck.

"I got you out. Your mom must've heard the crash and she came running, and I told her to call nine-one-one. After that it was cops, paramedics, detectives, the whole nine yards."

"Where's Sarah? Is she okay?"

"She's fine. She's at home with your mom. They wanted to come here, but I told them you were okay and to stay put."

"You're sure they're okay?" He nodded, and I processed this for a few seconds. "Wait a second, wait a second, I remember something," I said. "You were arguing with Detective Jakes."

"Right. He was being an asshole and I told him so. The paramedics were on my side."

"Where is Jakes?"

"Outside with his partner, waiting to see if you'll wake up."

"My head hurts." I probed the back of my head and found a lump. "Somebody hit me."

"Right."

"No, I'm serious," I said. "Somebody hit me."

"I believe you."

I didn't like the emphasis he put on the word "I."

"What do you mean? Did I hear the word . . . 'suicide' as I was waking up?"

He winced.

"You heard that, huh? I was reaming those two nurses—," he started to explain.

"Who said anything about suicide, Paul?"

"The nurses were talking at your door and one of them said they heard that you tried to commit suicide."

"What? Heard from who?"

"That's what I was trying to find out when you woke up."

He grabbed my hand and held it tightly.

"You scared the shit out of me," he said. "When I went into your garage I thought . . . I thought you were . . ."

It would have been very touching if I hadn't been so angry.

"I want to know who said anything about suicide," I insisted.

"So do I."

"Let Jakes and Davis in here."

"Are you sure? We can put it off until tomorrow, when you're feeling—"

"I want to do this now, before the story gets out about a suicide attempt."

He winced again.

"What?"

"Might be too late for that. There were newspaper people here when we pulled up."

"Great. If the nurses told them what they heard, I'll be tabloid fodder for days. Let's hope we can nip this in the bud, Paul. Let the detectives in."

"If you're sure—"

"I'm fine!" I realized I was being too strident with him. "I'm fine," I said again, softer this time, and I squeezed his hand. Men like it when you squeeze their hand. "Can we turn on some lights?"

"Sure," he said. "I'll go and get the detectives. But I'm staying while you talk to them," he added firmly.

"Good," I said, "I wouldn't have it any other way."

# Chapter 27

Jakes and Davis came back in with Paul. The nurse was nowhere in sight. I guess there were no visiting hour limitations for cops.

"Ms. Peterson," Jakes said, "I'm glad you're feeling better."

"Somewhat," I said, rubbing my head.

"Would you like to tell us what happened?"

"Somebody tried to kill me," I said, "and apparently, they were trying to make it look like a suicide. Wouldn't that have made me look guilty, Detective?"

"Yes, ma'am," he said. "Very guilty."

"The nurses were talking about my trying to commit suicide. That's going to show up in the papers tomorrow. I don't like being tabloid fodder, Detective."

"I'm sure it was just a case of conjecture on someone's part, Alex," he said, spreading his hands. "And if you didn't like being tabloid fodder, wouldn't you be better off in another business?"

"And if you didn't like eating donuts, wouldn't you be in another business?"

Paul chuckled, and even Davis laughed and said, "She got you there, partner."

Jakes turned on Davis then and said, "You know, I'm getting goddamned sick and tired of you taking her side all the time just because you're a fuckin' soap opera junkie, Len."

Davis's face got red, and I thought he was going to jump right back into Jakes's face, but instead he said, "I'll be out in the hall, *partner*."

Then Jakes turned on me.

"If it turns up in the tabloids tomorrow that you tried to commit suicide, don't blame me, Ms. Peterson. There were a lot of people at the scene, including your boyfriend, here."

"What the fuck?" Paul said. "Don't get in my face, Detective. I won't back down from you the way your partner did."

"For your information, my partner didn't back down," Jakes said, defending Davis's actions. "He's gonna ream my ass when we get back to the car. He doesn't like public displays of affection."

"Well, I don't have that problem with public displays," Paul shot back, his jaw jutting out, "so bring it on."

The two men faced each other with their chins almost touching, and I diffused the situation by applauding. They both looked at me.

"Okay, the lady is impressed, gentlemen. Now, why don't the two of you take it out into the hall. I have a splitting headache and my throat hurts. I'm done talking for today."

They both started to protest, but I held up my hand and waggled my forefinger at them.

"Done talking," I said, "to either of you. Now . . . go."

Jakes looked annoyed, while Paul looked hurt. I actually was impressed by Paul holding his own with Jakes, but I'd let him know about it another time. At that moment I wanted everybody out of my room.

"I'll see you in the morning," Paul said.

"Okay."

He leaned over and kissed my forehead. I didn't like that under normal circumstances. It made me feel like a little girl. But in this instance I didn't like it because it was proprietary. He was marking his territory in front of Jakes. Why that should have bothered me I didn't know. I didn't have the least bit of feeling for Jakes as a man, only as a cop—and an annoying one, at that.

They both left and I helped myself to another cup of water. After that I reached for the buzzer and pressed it for the nurse. She appeared almost immediately. I wondered what I had done—or what anyone had done—to rate me that kind of response time.

"What can I do for you, sweetie?"

I wanted to tell her she could start by not calling me sweetie, but apparently she was my contact with the outside world.

"Can you tell me how long I'll have to stay here?"

"Probably only overnight," she said. "It's just a precaution."

"I'll bet I could go home right now," I said.

"You could," she agreed. "You could sign yourself out and walk out the front door, but I should warn you, there are still reporters out there. Staying here would at least give you a peaceful night."

How could I argue with that?

"Okay," I said, "thanks." As she started to leave I called out, "Oh, is the phone on?"

"Yes," she said, "it'll be on all night."

"Thank you."

As she left I grabbed the phone and dialed my mom's number. She answered the phone anxiously, and I had to assure her several times I was all right before she would put Sarah on the phone. I then had to assure my daughter that I'd be home the next day, and that she should go to sleep and stop worrying about her mom. She told me she'd go to sleep, but she would not stop worrying. I told her we had a deal, and how much I loved her.

I hung up the phone, my eyelids feeling very heavy.

The next thing I knew I woke up in darkness. I lay very still and waited for my eyes to adjust, then looked around the room. It wasn't a private room, but the other bed was empty. Some moonlight peeked in from between the closed blinds.

I could see the doorway clearly. It was closed, and there was a little light beneath it from the hall. I suddenly felt very vulnerable. If someone had tried to kill me—what was I thinking? Someone *had* tried to kill me and make it look like I wanted to commit suicide out of guilt. What was to stop them from trying again tonight, in the hospital?

So much for my peaceful night.

# Chapter 28

I sat up in bed and buzzed for the nurse. Spoiled because of her earlier response time, I became nervous when she didn't appear.

I wondered what had woken me. My throat was raw and I still had a headache, but I was starting to feel that I should have just checked myself out and gone home.

I didn't like the light being off, but I stopped myself just short of turning on the lamp that was right above my head. If somebody was coming to get me and they entered the room now, I'd be able to see, but they wouldn't. My eyes were used to the dark while theirs would have to adjust. Small advantage, but I'd take what I could get.

I rang for the nurse again. No answer. Now I was really nervous. I looked at the phone, but whom could I call who could help me in the next few minutes?

I was on my own.

I tossed back the sheet and swung my feet to the floor, which was ice cold. I was wearing one of those hospital gowns that open in the back, and I could feel the cold along my spine, as well, but I didn't think that was where my chill was coming from.

I stood up, feeling light-headed now as well as headachy. I suddenly realized I was hungry. Never let it be said fear interfered with my appetite.

Suddenly I saw something beneath the door, a shadow—two feet. My heart leaped into my throat and I looked around for a weapon. All I could come up with was a bedpan, but it was metal so I grabbed it and moved quietly toward the door.

I held the bedpan over my head and waited. The door opened slowly and I realized I'd been wrong about me being the only one who could see. Light from the hall streamed in and illuminated the bed, which was, of course, empty because I was behind the door with my bedpan held high, my hospital gown gaping in the back and the soles of my feet feeling like ice.

"Ms. Peterson?" a man said.

I started to bring the bedpan down when I saw clearly by the light from the hall that the man was wearing a policeman's uniform.

"Oh God," I said.

He turned toward me, startled.

"Ma'am?" he asked. "Are you all right?"

He reached out and caught me or I would have fallen. . . .

When I woke up I was back in bed with both the nurse and the policeman standing next to me.

"Now, honey, what were you trying to do?" the nurse asked.

"I buzzed," I said, weakly. "You didn't come right away. . . ."

"I just stepped away from the desk for a minute," she explained.

"I—I thought someone was . . . was coming after me. . . ."

"But you had a policeman stationed at your door," she said. "Didn't they tell you?"

"No," I said, feeling stronger—and madder—"they didn't."

"Ma'am, I'm sorry," the cop said. He had his hat off, revealing a head of steel wool–looking gray hair. I wondered how close to retirement he was. "I—I was just opening the door to check on you."

"No, I'm sorry," I said. "I almost clobbered you with a—a bedpan."

"I don't think you're strong enough to hurt me, even with that pan," he said. "I caught you when you fainted and put you back in bed."

I could feel my face flush bright red. Just how open had my gown been in the back?

"Honest, ma'am," he said, reading my look correctly, "I didn't see . . . or touch . . . a thing."

"It's all right," I told him. "I just feel . . . so silly."

"Well, to tell you the truth, Ms. Peterson," he said, smiling suddenly, "you looked kinda silly holdin' that bedpan over your head."

"Yeah," I said, giving him a wan smile, "I suppose I did."

"Do you want something to help you sleep, honey?" the nurse asked.

"No," I said, "I'll be all right." I looked at the cop.

His name tag said WILSON. "Officer Wilson, will you be outside my door all night?"

"Until I'm relieved in the morning, Ms. Peterson," he said, "or until you leave the hospital."

"Did the detectives say they'd be back in the morning?"

"I believe they did."

"Thank you," I said. "Thank you both. I'll be fine now."

Just go, I wanted to say, but I didn't and they went anyway, turning out the light on the way out.

Paul was coming back in the morning, and so were the detectives. I wondered if I could get myself signed out before any of them arrived.

# Chapter 29

When I awoke the next morning my headache was gone, but my throat still felt a little raw. There also seemed to be a burning sensation in my nostrils. I realized that I had not spoken to a doctor at all. The clock on the table next to my bed told me it was eight thirty a.m. I had a choice. I could get up, get dressed—assuming my clothes were somewhere in that room—and get out of there before any of the men showed up to pester me, or I could buzz for the nurse and ask to see the doctor. Did I want to know how close I actually came to dying? And how long my nose and throat would feel this way?

And who the hell tried to kill me?

I sat up straight. Why hadn't I been wondering that all night? Somebody had conked me on the head, stuck me in my car and tried to gas me. (I know, it wasn't gas; it was carbon monoxide.)

The realization that someone tried to kill me was followed closely by another. I had scared someone into action. One of the people I spoke to was the killer, and now they had tried to kill me and were trying to make it seem as if I was the killer.

Paul walked in at that moment and I said, "I'm being framed."

"I know that," he said. "I know you didn't try to kill yourself."

"No," I said, as he took my hand, "I mean from the beginning. I was being framed for Marcy's murder."

I explained my thoughts to him and he listened intently before offering an opinion.

"Your logic is not completely sound," he said.

"Why not?"

"First, it's not necessarily someone who you've spoken to over the past few days," he said. "It could be someone they've spoken to."

"I see. The word could've simply gotten around that I was asking questions."

"Yes."

"What else?"

"Well, second, you're certainly right that you're being framed, but the frame doesn't have to have been in place from the beginning," he said. "It could have been added later."

"I get it," I said, putting the brakes on my enthusiasm. Once that was done, though, I still had my fear. "They could have decided to frame me because I found the body. . . ."

"And because you fit."

Detectives Jakes and Davis walked in at that point, Jakes with a big smile on his face.

"Alex," he said, "you're looking much better."

"I feel better," I said. "Ready to go home."

"Have you talked to a doctor yet?" Paul asked.

"No, but—"

"I think you should do that before we leave, don't you?"

"Makes sense to me," Jakes said to Paul. "We'd be very happy to keep Alex company while you go and find her doctor, Mr. Silas."

"Now look—"

"It's okay, Paul," I said. "Go on. I'll talk with the detectives."

He was reluctant to leave me with Jakes—and Davis—but finally went in search of the doctor.

"Can you remember what happened yesterday?" Jakes asked.

"Some of it."

I told them everything I could remember, and then they started asking more questions.

"Did you see anyone?"

"No," I said then. "Not clearly. I saw . . . a shape."

"Man or woman?"

"A . . . large shape," I said. "And I got the impression of . . . strength, when I was lifted."

"So it was probably a man," Davis said.

"Or a very strong woman," Jakes said.

"Was there anything in the newspaper this morning?" I asked.

Jakes and Davis exchanged a look.

"What?"

"It won't make you happy."

"Tell me."

"Mmm, something along the lines of 'Soap Opera Diva in Probable Suicide Attempt,'" Jakes said.

I hesitated a moment, letting it sink in, then said, "Diva? They said diva?"

"Unfair," Davis said.

"Yes," Jakes agreed, "very unfair. I don't find anything divalike about you, Alex."

"Thank you!" I looked at him earnestly. "I hate that word. Why can't I just be referred to as an actress? They actually called me a diva? Unbelievable!"

I was harping on the word "diva," but I was really pissed about the suicide part.

"Alex," Jakes said, "I want to help you."

"Why? Don't you still consider me a suspect?"

"Well, yes . . ."

"Even after what happened?"

"I'm a policeman, Alex," he said. "I have to suspect everyone. What happened last night, there's still a small possibility it was a suicide attempt—or set up to look like one. Or maybe you want it to look like someone tried to make it seem like you were trying to commit suicide—"

"Wait, wait, wait," I said, holding up my hands and then grabbing my head. "What?" I looked past him at Davis. "Do you understand what he's saying?"

"All he's trying to say is—"

"I can explain myself, Detective Davis," Jakes said.

"Not doing such a good job of it so far, Jakes," I goaded.

We glared at each other for a few moments and I was really proud of myself that I didn't look away. Then Paul entered with a man in white.

"I'm Dr. Glenn," he said. "Am I interrupting something?"

"An interrogation, Doctor," Jakes said. "We're just trying—"

"I can't allow you to do that until I've examined her," the doctor said. "I want you and your partner out of here."

"Doctor—"

"Now!"

Jakes firmed his jaw; then Davis put his hand on his partner's arm.

"We'll be in the visitor's lounge," Jakes said, and the two of them turned and left.

# Chapter 30

The doctor looked at Paul and asked, "Was that good enough?"

"Excellent, Doctor," Paul said. "I couldn't have asked for more."

"You two cooked that up just to get rid of them?" I asked.

"Mr. Silas did the cooking," the doctor said. "I simply agreed to go along, but now . . . Mr. Silas, I'm afraid you have to leave, as well."

"What?"

"I really do need to examine Ms. Peterson before I can discharge her."

"Oh," Paul said, "well then . . . I guess I'll wait outside."

The doctor nodded. Paul smiled at me reassuringly and left. Dr. Glenn looked to be in his forties, with a silly pointed goatee that looked even sillier because there was no mustache.

"Dr. Glenn," I said, as he prepared to check me over, "were you the one who examined me when I came in last night?"

"Yes."

"What was my condition?"

"You exhibited all the symptoms of carbon monoxide poisoning," he said, while checking my eyes with a small flashlight. "You complained of headache and dizziness. You were disoriented, short of breath, confused. You were also hallucinating."

"Hallucinating?"

"You claimed someone tried to kill you."

I slapped his hand away from my face.

"Someone *did* try to kill me."

"That's not for me to decide," he said. "I simply treated you for carbon monoxide poisoning. You also vomited and complained of chest pains."

"What about the bump on my head?"

"That was minor. You probably hit your head when your boyfriend pulled you out of the car, or carried you out of the garage."

"Minor? Somebody knocked me unconscious."

"I don't think so."

"I do."

He smiled a very professional smile.

"As I said, you were hallucinating."

"Are you saying that the blow to the back of my head that gave me this bump did not knock me out?"

Now he looked annoyed. He put his hands to the back of my head, found the lump and probed.

"I suppose. . . ."

"You suppose? Didn't you take it into account last night? This kind of bump could not have come from just accidentally bumping my head. It's more consistent with a blow from a blunt instrument."

"Well," he admitted, rather sheepishly, "I didn't really see this last night. . . ."

"What?" I couldn't believe what I was hearing. "You didn't find the bump on my head."

"You were brought in as a probable suicide attempt," he explained. "You exhibited all the symptoms. There was no reason to—"

"Wait a minute, wait a minute," I said, holding my hands out in front of me. "Get away from me."

"What?"

"Back away from me!" I shouted. "Paul! Paul!" I was hoping he was right outside.

He came running in, a look of concern on his face.

"What's wrong?"

"Get this quack away from me," I said, "and get me my clothes. I'm getting out of here!"

"What did you do to her?" Paul asked.

The doctor waved his arms helplessly.

"I—I didn't do anything—"

"He sure didn't," I said, getting out of bed. "That looks like it might be a closet, Paul. Check it for me, will you?"

"Sure." He started for the closet.

"But first get him out of here," I said.

"I have to examine—"

"Get . . . him . . . out!"

Paul approached the doctor.

"You better leave."

The doctor looked aggrieved.

"All right," he said. "I—I'll have someone else come in and examine her."

"Fine," Paul said. "Just leave."

He left.

Paul went to the closet and came back with my clothes."

"Close the door," I told him.

"I'm not sure I like this new bossy you, Alex," he said, but he did what I told him.

At the door he asked, "You want to tell me why I kicked the doctor out of your hospital room?"

"He's the one who examined me when I came in last night," I said, turning my back so I could pull on my pants and sweater. "He didn't find the bump on the back of my head."

"So that means—"

"They admitted me as a probable suicide. That's why it's in the papers."

"Oh, you saw that?"

"No, but Jakes told me about it. Are my shoes in there?"

He went over, took a look, picked them up from the floor and brought them to me. I sat on the bed and slipped my thongs on.

"So what are you going to do?" he asked.

"Get the hell out of here."

I stood up, wavered and would have fallen if he hadn't grabbed me.

"Are you all right?"

"Dizziness," I said. "One of the symptoms." I didn't mention confusion and hallucinations. "I'm fine. Let's get out of here."

"Jakes and his partner are going to be looking for you," he said.

"Let them come and find me," I said. "I want out of here, Paul. Are you going to help me?"

"We can go to the front desk and sign you out—"

"To hell with signing out," I said. "I just want to go. I don't want to see cops, and I don't want to see the press, who probably camped out front."

"I can't talk you out of this?"

"Why would you want to?"

"Alex—"

"Paul, you've been wanting to help me for a long time," I said. "Now I'm asking."

He stared at me for a few moments, then said, "Okay, then. Let's get out of here."

# Chapter 31

Paul got me down the hall, away from the lounge, and out a back exit to his car. We managed to avoid all cops, doctors, nurses and press. We did run into an orderly or two, but they had no reason to stop us. They'd also probably remember us, and tell Detective Jakes—when asked.

In the front seat of Paul's car I released the breath I'd been holding since we'd left the room. I kept expecting to hear Jakes shouting at us to halt, or come back.

"You all right?" Paul asked.

"Not yet," I said, leaning back against the headrest, "but it would help to get far away from here."

"To where?"

"I have to hug Sarah."

"Then home it is."

"Wait. The paparazzi. I can't go home. But I really need to."

Paul pulled out his cell and called my house.

"Charlotte, take Sarah and get in the car. Try not to run over anyone. . . . I know. Meet us at the restaurant down the street . . . IHOP. Okay . . . Ten minutes. Oh, and bring Alex a change of clothes . . . sweats?" He looked at me and I nodded. "Yeah, sweats will be fine. See you in a few." He pressed END.

I looked at Paul and my eyes started to well up.

"Thank you. You're really good to have around—did you know that?"

He touched my face and said simply, "You're welcome."

We pulled up to the restaurant and my mom and daughter were already there. Sarah jumped up out of her seat and into my arms.

"Momma, Momma where's your booboo?"

My mom chimed in with, "Alex, how are you? Let me see you." They both were talking at the same time.

We moved back into the restaurant where I hugged and kissed them.

"I'm really okay, you guys! Just a little groggy."

"You need to be in bed, Alex!" my mom said. "How could the hospital let you out?"

I took her aside.

"Mom, you're probably right. But I can't go home and they were making me crazy at the hospital. I have something I have to do."

"But . . . Alex . . . ," she interjected.

"Mom . . . please. Take care of Sarah. I'll call you and keep you updated."

After spending some time assuring them I was fine, I kissed Sarah a million times and watched them go out the door and get in the car. Breathing a heavy sigh, I looked at Paul.

"What the hell is going on, Paul? When do I get my life back?"

"Why don't you go freshen up in the ladies' room and we'll talk about it?"

I grabbed the sweats my mom had brought and made a beeline for the bathroom.

"Be right back."

I needed a lot of freshening up, so by the time I got back to the table there was already a cheese omelet, toast and a hot pot of coffee waiting for me. In spite of the fact that someone had tried to kill me, and my throat still felt a little raw, I was starving.

"They admitted me to that hospital," I said, while we ate, "as a suicide. No one even did a full examination of me or they would have found the bump on my head. No wonder Jakes and Davis were looking at me funny. If it had been on my chart it would have been a different story. And I certainly wouldn't be in the papers today." I scanned the room.

"What are you looking for?" he asked.

"I want to see if anybody has today's paper."

"Let's worry about that later, Alex," he said. "Running out of the hospital, avoiding Jakes and his partner is not going to convince them that what you're saying is true."

"You're right," I said, "but finding the son of a bitch who hit me is."

"And how do we find him?" he asked. "And was it a he?"

"I was disoriented," I said, "but I get the distinct impression it was a he." It would have taken a pretty strong woman to lift me and put me behind the wheel, and I haven't talked to any women that big and strong."

"And men?"

"I've talked to a lot of men, and they all could've done it."

"Okay," he said, "so you and I have to go back over the men you talked to. Tell me what you said to them, what they said to you and what their attitude was."

"I can do that," I said. "I remember all my conversations."

"We're going to have to try to figure out which one of them had a motive to kill Marcy," he explained, "and a motive to frame you, and *then* a reason to try to kill you now."

"And I can't go back home," I said. "The cops will be looking for me there. And the press . . ."

"Alex, I don't know if it's such a good idea to avoid the cops—"

"Look, screw them, Paul," I said. "Let them come and find me. I have to be out here trying to clear my name, not lying in the hospital like some poor, pathetic attempted suicide."

"Okay," Paul said, "okay. Well, let's start now. Later we can find a place for you to stay. You can stay with me. Bring Sarah and your mom."

"They'll look there."

"All right, then," he said, "we'll deal with that later. Right now let's start from the beginning and you tell me about the men you've talked to."

*     *     *

We sat there for a couple of hours and got a second pot of coffee. My headache came back and I wished I had some Tylenol or something, but I pushed through.

"You know," Paul said, when I was done, "I think I'd key on the daughter."

"Why?"

"It sounds to me like she had something she wanted to tell you. And then there's the husband. Husband or ex, he's usually the guilty party in a case like this. It makes more sense to me than some disgruntled actor from work killing her over some real or imagined slight in a soap script."

"You don't know how deeply invested these people are in their characters," I told him. "If you're not being written for at all or written for badly, that could make the difference between having a job on a soap or waiting tables. A simple change in a story line could mean a complete change in an actor's bank account and quality of life. I've seen it happen time and time again. And it's not fun. It could have and still could happen to me. How far would someone go to hold on to a modicum of celebrity and a substantial source of income? People have killed for far less, believe me."

"I guess you're right. So, I think our next move is to go talk to the husband and daughter again. If we're lucky you'll be able to get the daughter alone."

"Julia."

"What?"

"Her name is Julia."

"Okay," he said, "let's talk to Julia. You said they lived in Malibu?"

"Yes."

"Let's go, then."

I got up from the table slowly. I had the feeling if I got up too fast I'd pass out. My head had started pounding again.

"Are you sure you're up to this, Alex?" he asked, reaching out to support me.

"I'm up to it," I said, "but can we stop along the way for some Extra Strength Tylenol?"

# Chapter 32

The front gate was open. I might have thought something was wrong, except that it was open the last time I was there, too.

"I thought these people were fanatics about their privacy?" Paul said, driving through the gate and up the drive. "That's why they live here."

"I guess Henry Roswell is not that private a person," I said.

We drove up to the front of the house, parked behind a black Lexus and got out. I tried the front door, just to see what would happen, but it was locked.

"We could go around the back and get in on the beach side," I said.

"I don't want to break and enter, Alex," Paul said. "We just want to talk to the guy and his daughter."

"Fine," I said, trying to cover my nervousness, "don't be any fun. See if I care."

The painkiller was working on my headache already, and I felt better.

Paul rang the bell and we waited; then he rang it again.

"Can they hear this if they're out back?" he asked.

"I don't know," I said. "Certainly not if they're on the beach."

"Is that Lexus his car?"

"I don't know," I said. "I guess so, or it could be Julia's."

"Okay," he said, "let's go around back, but I still don't want to break in."

"Fine."

We walked around the house, taking the opportunity to peer into a window or two along the way, but nothing was moving.

When we got to the back I walked to the stairs and tried to see the beach, but it was out of view. We could see farther to the right and left, but not directly below us.

"Alex?"

I turned. Paul was standing in front of the sliding glass doors.

"They're open," he said.

"Would going in constitute breaking and entering?" I asked.

"Well, maybe not in the strictest sense of the phrase," he said. "After all, we're not actually breaking— we're just entering. . . ."

I walked over and joined him in front of the door. On the way I saw something on the tiles outside. A spot—a red one, very smooth around the edges, about the size of a dime. I crouched down, studied it, then touched it with my finger. Tacky. It was blood.

"Paul?"

He walked over to me and looked down. I pointed

to the spot. It was perfectly round. He stood next to me and studied it.

"Well, Mr. Forensics?" I asked. "Did somebody get killed out here so neatly that only one spot of blood fell?"

"It's round," he said. "It's more in line with a nosebleed—or like a spot of paint that simply dropped from a brush."

"It is blood, right?"

He crouched down, didn't touch it but examined it as closely as he could.

"It's blood, all right. Good catch, Alex."

He stood up.

"Let's go inside."

"Paul—"

"We can't call the police because we saw one drop of blood."

"I don't want to call the police at all."

"Well then, let's go inside and see if we can wake somebody up. But let's go carefully."

That was true enough. It wasn't noon yet, and some people did sleep that late. I'd heard about it on the news, but never got to experience it myself.

Paul went first and I followed. He pursed his lips and gave a low whistle. I had been there before, so I knew the house was whistle worthy.

"Hello?" Paul called.

Nothing.

We moved farther into the house and he shouted, "Anybody home?"

No answer.

"Should we split up?" I asked.

"No," he said, taking my hand, "I'm not letting you out of my sight."

I squeezed his hand, this time because I wanted to.

"Bedrooms must be upstairs," Paul said. "There's got to be a den or an office or something down here. Any ideas?"

"All I saw was the back, and then a walk-through," I said.

"Let's look around. I suggest we start upstairs so we don't get any surprises."

We went up and checked the bedrooms. They were empty, and the beds were made. There were no drops of blood anywhere. We checked closets and looked under the beds.

"Okay," Paul said, "nobody's up here, whether or not they belong. Let's check downstairs."

As we did I kept looking at the floor for more blood spots, but there were none. I hoped that was a good sign.

We peeked into a couple of rooms and found the one where Henry worked on his physique. The kind of stuff people who bought all those Something-flexes from the TV infomercials wished they could afford.

And then we found what we were looking for at the end of a hallway. An office, complete with bookshelves, file cabinets and a desk.

"Okay," Paul said, "there's nobody home and the back door is wide-open. They've either gone for a swim or . . ."

"They didn't strike me as the kind of father/daughter who went for swims together."

"Then something's wrong."

"Past experience tells me we should look under the desk."

"Good idea." He started forward, then stopped and looked at me. "Coming?"

As I dashed past him I said, "Coming. Of course I'm coming."

We moved forward slowly, eventually working our way around behind the desk. Bare legs and part of a bathrobe were the first things I saw. And a large pool of blood. Very large. It was Henry, all right, and he was dead.

Not again.

# Chapter 33

I bent down to get a closer look and Paul grabbed my arm, pulling me back.

"Stop, Alex! You don't want to compromise the crime scene!"

"I just wanted . . ."

"Try to control yourself. This isn't fun and games." Paul had a point. I had to get past my innate curiosity about all things dead and focus on the big picture. This poor guy had been a living, breathing human being. A father, someone's son. Get a grip, Alex! Get your ass into therapy, maybe.

"Okay, so what do we do now?" I asked. I felt as if my feet were rooted to the floor.

"We call the police."

"The very people I'm trying to avoid."

"Do you want me to call them and tell them I found the body?"

"No," I said, shaking my head, "no, don't do that. We'll talk to them together."

He reached for his cell phone.

"Wait," I said.

"For what?"

"We have an opportunity here," I said. "You're the expert. You have a chance to examine the scene."

"Alex—"

"They're not going to let you do it, Paul," I said. "They're going to kick us both out."

He frowned, looked at his phone, then put it away.

"Okay," he said, "a quick look."

We both crouched down to look at Henry.

"Is this how Marcy was when you found her?" he asked.

"Yes."

He reached out with one finger and probed the body.

"Still warm, no rigor."

"Like Marcy."

He nodded and we stood up. The top of the desk was a mess, as if someone had swept an arm across it. Some of the stuff was on the floor—a paperweight, pens and pencils. A laptop, which had been knocked askew, was perched precariously on the edge.

"Could've been a struggle," Paul said, falling into professional mode.

"What about a weapon?" I asked. "Marcy's Emmy was under the desk with her."

"There's no lamp on the desk," Paul said, pointing, "but there is a round circle in the dust, here."

We crouched down again. There it was, underneath Henry, a lamp with a round iron base, the kind that extended and had a hinge so it could be adjusted. The kind that could have been picked up and swung.

"So there was a fight, and the killer picked up the lamp and hit him."

"Same as Marcy."

"Probably. Could be two different killers, though. Could be a coincidence that both exes were killed the same week."

"Could be," I asked, "but how likely is it?"

"Not very. Okay, let's get out of here into another room and call the cops."

"At least we know that everything is similar to what I saw in Marcy's office when I found her," I said as we left. "It's got to be the same killer."

"I agree."

"And I'd have no motive to kill her ex-husband," I said. "I didn't even know he existed until this week."

We left the room, careful not to touch anything. We left the door open, as we had found it.

We walked through the house until we reached the kitchen, where he took out his cell phone again. He was about to pick it up when we heard something.

"What was that?" he asked.

"And where did it come from?"

We stood very still, and heard it again. It sounded like somebody crying.

"That door must lead to the garage," Paul said, pointing.

"That one might be a closet," I said, pointing the other way.

We each went to our chosen door and opened it. Mine was empty except for cleaning stuff—broom, mop, pail, rubber gloves, vacuum cleaner—plus an ironing board and shelves with closet stuff on them such as plastic drinking cups, cleaning fluids, detergents, towels and rags.

I closed the door and turned around. Paul was coming back in from the garage.

"There's a nice silver Mercedes in there, but that's all."

We heard the crying again. This time we both looked at the marble-topped island that dominated the center of the room. There were doors underneath and we headed for it. When we opened the last one we found her, all curled up with her head down on her arms.

"Julia?"

She didn't move—just stayed there, sobbing.

"Julia, it's okay." I reached in and touched her arms. "Come on, it's Alex. Come on out."

She unfolded, stuck her legs out and then scooted. She was wearing jeans and a sweatshirt, no shoes. Paul helped her to her feet, and she fell against me, shivering and crying.

"She's scared stiff, Paul," I said. "You call the police while I try to calm her down. Maybe I can find out what happened."

"Right."

"Come on, sweetie," I said. "Let's go into the living room."

"No, no," she said, pulling away, "they might still be here."

"Who?" I asked. "Who might still be here?"

"I don't know," she said. "Whoever killed my dad."

"You know your dad is dead?"

She nodded.

"I—I heard them."

"Heard them killing him?"

Paul was talking into the phone and looking over at us.

"Julia, come with me," I said. "No one is here. We checked the whole house. It's safe."

I put my arm around her shoulders and led her from the kitchen to the living room, where we sat on a big sofa.

"Now Julia, tell me what you heard."

"My dad was arguing with somebody in his office," she said. "They were yelling. . . ."

"Could you hear anything they were saying?"

"N-no," she said. "No. I was . . . afraid. I don't . . . I don't like violence. It . . . scares me."

I wondered how this kid got to be her age and so skittish. The way the world was today, the way kids were, I was surprised. Most girls her age are already jaded.

"So you hid?"

"Yes," she said. "I didn't want them to find me."

"Do you know how many there were?"

She shook her head.

"I'm such a coward," she said. "I shoulda helped my dad."

"Julia," I asked, "you didn't see the person arrive? Didn't hear the bell?"

"I came in from outside," she said. "I was walking on the beach. When I got back the sliding glass doors were open, and when I came in I—I heard them yelling. I—I think I heard them fighting."

"Julia, how did you know your dad was dead?"

"I don't know," she said. "Somebody killed my mom, so I guess I just thought—"

"The cops are on their way," Paul said, entering the living room. "I told them to notify Jakes and Davis."

I must have given him a dirty look, because he put his hands up in apology and sat down on a chair.

"I—I don't want to talk about this anymore," Julia said. She turned her tear-streaked face to me. "What am I gonna do, Alex? I'm all alone."

"Don't you have any relatives? Aunts or uncles?"

"My dad has a sister back east, but they don't talk. Haven't for years. I—I couldn't call her."

"Well," I said, "we'll worry about that later. Julia, the police will be here soon and you'll have to talk to them—"

She grabbed my hands and gripped them tightly.

"You won't leave me, will you, Alex?"

"I—I don't know if they'll let me stay—"

"I won't talk to them if they make you leave," she said. "I won't."

I couldn't tell her that Jakes might put me in handcuffs right away. Maybe her dependence on me would put that off for a while.

"All right," I said, "all right, we'll make them let me stay."

In the distance I could hear a siren.

# Chapter 34

Two patrol cops arrived first; Paul talked to them and showed them the body. One of them stayed with it while the other one waited at the front door for the detectives. When Jakes and Davis arrived, Jakes looked over at me and shook his head. Then he and his partner went to look at the body. They took Paul with them, leaving the one officer at the front door. When Jakes returned he was alone—minus his partner and without Paul.

"Alex," he said, "sorry we missed you at the hospital this morning. We must have got our signals crossed."

"Yes," I said, "we must've." Was that all he was going to say?

"Would you introduce me to the young lady?" he asked.

"Detective Jakes, this is Julia Roswell."

"Julia," Jakes said, "I understand you've had a rough time of it lately, but if I'm going to catch whoever killed your mother and your father, I'll need your help."

"W-what can I do?" she asked.

"Well, for one thing, you can talk to me," he said, gently. "Can you do that?"

Julia underwent an amazing transformation right in front of me. She went from weepy child to smitten young woman.

"Of course," she told him, pulling away from me. "I can do that."

"Good. Alex?"

I looked at him, then took the hint.

"Oh, sure," I said. "I'll, uh, go make some coffee, since we're probably to have still more people traipsing through here." I looked at Jakes. "Can I do that?"

"If all you touch is what you need to make coffee," he said, taking the seat I had just vacated. That put him right next to Julia, who ran her fingers through her hair and then sat primly with her hands clasped between her knees.

So much for wanting me around.

"Now Julia," I heard him saying as I walked away, "why don't we just start at the beginning, huh, sweetheart? How old are you, by the way . . . ?"

Julia wasn't the only one who had undergone a transformation. I was shocked at how gentle Jakes was being with her, and I knew it was both that gentleness and his good looks that had managed to put Julia at ease with him. I should have been glad, but it irritated me. Why was he so abrasive with me? Or was he? Maybe it was just my perception of him, but he always seemed on the verge of sarcasm, even down to the way he said my name.

The kitchen filled with the aroma of coffee. I'd

found a special blend in the cabinet. It was something Henry Roswell had ground for himself at a coffee shop I'd never heard of.

While I was waiting for it to brew I decided to snoop some more. I had put on a pair of the rubber gloves just to be on the safe side, so I started opening drawers and more cabinets. I even studied the notepad and magnets on the refrigerator.

"That smells good."

I turned and saw Davis standing there.

"Is it ready?"

"Oh, sure," I said. "How do you take it?"

"Just black," he said. "Good coffee should always be drunk black."

I poured the coffee into a heavy cardboard mug I'd found in the cupboard, behind the plastic ones. I wondered about a rich man who has special coffee blended for him, then keeps disposable cups in his cupboard.

"Looking for clues?" he asked, with an amused look on his face.

His attitude made me mad.

"I seem to be the one finding the bodies." I said. "Why not the clues, too?"

"Touché, Ms. Peterson."

"You can call me Alex, Detective," I said.

"Actually," he said, "you're more Tiffany to me."

"Okay," I said, "I'll settle for Ms. Peterson. Your partner is amazing with Julia. She wasn't going to talk to any cops without me. Now look at her."

"He has a way with, uh, women," Davis said.

"Really?" I asked. "I hadn't noticed that, myself."

"The man is an acquired taste."

"Even for you?" I asked. "Did you become partners just recently?"

"No," Davis said. "We've been partners for five years."

"Really?" Another surprise. "And he didn't know your child's name?"

Davis smiled.

"He knows it," Davis said. "He never forgets anything."

"You sound like you admire him."

"He's a great detective," Davis said.

"And you're not?"

"I'm a good cop," Davis said, and let it go at that. "Can we talk?"

"About what?"

He smiled and gestured toward the office with his cardboard mug, saying, "That."

"Oh," I said, and then realized he'd been putting me at ease before he questioned me.

I had the feeling that Detective Davis was much more than just a good cop. In fact, I was learning more about both of them.

Others came into the kitchen looking for the coffee, including Paul, the cop at the door, some of the technical people and even the man from the medical examiner's office. In between pouring coffee for them I answered Davis's questions.

No, I hadn't heard anything from inside the house when we arrived.

Yes, I did see something unusual, the drop of blood outside, in the back.

No, I hadn't noticed any movement when we entered the house through the already-open door.

Yes, I had met the man before, but he hadn't said anything to me to indicate he feared for his life.

Yes, I had met the daughter before—at the same time—and no, she didn't tell me anything he should know. (I decided not to tell Detective Davis that Julia told me she was glad her mother was dead.)

"Alex," he said, "why did you run out of the hospital today?"

I told him about the quack doctor who hadn't even bothered to check me for any injuries when he examined me the night before, but simply assumed I was an attempted suicide.

"I guess that would piss me off, too."

"Do you want to feel the bump?"

"Huh? Oh, no, no," he said, nervously. I realized that at that moment he was thinking of me as Tiffany again. "I'm sure it's there."

"Which means somebody hit me on the head and knocked me out."

He nodded and said, "Well, that's one thing it could mean."

"What else could it mean?"

"Maybe that you hit your head by accident or maybe that you did it on purpose."

"I hit myself on the head on purpose?"

I raised my voice to the point that several men in the other room turned to look, as did Jakes and Julia from the sofa.

"Tiff—uh, Ms. Peterson," Davis said, keeping his

voice low, "we're just talking about some possibilities, here."

"And do you think it's a possibility that I killed Henry Roswell last night?" I hissed at him.

"Of course not," he said. "You were in the hospital with a man on your door."

Who, I suddenly realized, had been put there to keep me in, not to keep anyone out.

"Well," I said, "thank God for small favors."

# Chapter 35

They were far from finished with the crime scene a couple of hours later, but apparently finished with me. And Julia.

Jakes came to talk to me in the kitchen. I couldn't complain about being relegated to coffee duty because number one, I volunteered, and number two, I knew I was not a suspect in this particular murder.

"Alex," Jakes said, "I should take you in for running out of the hospital that way."

"Why?" I asked. "I had every right to sign myself out."

"But you didn't sign yourself out. You snuck out the back door."

I waved my hand. "A technicality."

"You're a pain in the ass, you know that?"

"Detective," I said, "I've been called far worse in my life. That might be the nicest thing you've ever said to me."

My hand was on the countertop. He moved his hand over it and said, "I need to ask you a favor."

I was startled by this unlikely intimacy, but for some reason left my hand there. His skin felt warm and smooth. I wondered if the rest of him was the same. Before I had too much time to think about it Paul walked in, and I quickly snatched my hand away.

"Am I interrupting something?" he asked.

I swear I blushed. It's a curse. I've been a blusher my whole life. Whenever I try to be cool, my red face betrays me.

"Detective Jakes was just going to ask me a favor," I said.

"Oh? What kind of a favor?"

"It's Julia," Jakes said. "She has no place to go."

"What? You want Alex to take her home with her?" Paul asked. "For Chrissake, you suspect her of killing the girl's mother."

"I think we can assume, after last night's incident, that she's off that list."

"Really?" I asked, surprised.

"Yes, really."

"You mean, you don't believe I tried to commit suicide, like that idiot doctor—"

"I pretty much figured out the idiot doctor on my own, Alex," Jakes said. "No, I don't think you tried to commit suicide. For one thing I think you're very smart, and if you had wanted to kill yourself, you would have succeeded."

"Detective," I said, fanning my face with my hands, "this rash of compliments—"

"Yeah, yeah," he said, interrupting me. "Look, I can take her to a hotel, but she's a kid. She's never stayed in a hotel alone—"

"Isn't she eighteen?" Paul asked. "She's of age. She can be on her own."

"If I could leave her here I would, but it's a crime scene. She can't stay here. Besides, I don't think she should be alone. She's still a child, and she may be in danger."

"How can you expect Alex—"

"I'll take her."

"What?" Paul asked.

"Thank you, Alex," Jakes said. "I'll go and get her, and then the three of you can leave."

As Jakes went off to get Julia, Paul went off on me.

"What are you doing? You don't have to be responsible for this girl—"

"She's scared, Paul."

"Didn't you hear what the man said? You're out of it. You're not a suspect anymore. You can walk away from this whole mess."

"No, I can't," I said. "Somebody tried to kill me, and they may try again."

"I'll stay at the house with you—"

"I think it would be better if Jakes put a cop on the house," I said, cutting him off. "I don't want anyone inside, scaring Sarah, or even Julia."

"You're saying I'd scare—"

"Paul, please don't argue with me," I said. "I just want to get out of here, get Julia out of here and go home to my daughter."

Paul was fuming, and I thought I knew why.

"What was . . . that all about?" he demanded.

"What?"

"You know what," he said. "The . . . flirting, the blushing . . . What's going on, Alex?"

"Paul, you're being silly. I wasn't flirting with any-one."

"That's not the way it looked to me."

"Are you going to harp on this all the way home, or should I call a cab?"

"You know what, Alex?" he said. "Maybe you should do that."

"Fine!"

"Fine!"

He turned and stormed off, and I bit my lip. I hadn't really picked a fight with him, but it seemed that I did manage to light his fuse. Did I do that on purpose?

Jakes came back to the kitchen with Julia and asked, "Where's Mr. Silas?"

"He had to leave."

"Do you need a ride home?" he asked.

"Yes, please." I looked at Julia. "You okay, kiddo?"

"I—I don't know," she said, with a shrug. It seemed her crush on Jakes had lifted her spirits for only so long.

"Let me just clear up a few things and I'll drive you home," Jakes said.

"Um, Detective, I'll need you to run interference with the press. Is there anything you can do to get rid of them?"

"I'd like nothing better." And he immediately pulled out his cell and started barking orders.

As he walked away Julia said, "I really don't want to be alone right now, but I don't have anywhere to go."

I was sure Julia had money of her own, certainly enough for a hotel, but I was equally sure she'd never been to a hotel alone. With no mother to raise her she probably had a doting father who spoiled her. Unprepared for the real world, she was suddenly thrust into it.

"That's okay," I said. "You can come home with me."

"But for how long?"

"We'll figure it out."

I looked over to where Jakes was talking to his partner, Davis, who seemed agitated. Jakes waved, pointed and then came walking back over to us.

"Problems?" I asked.

"No," Jakes said, "I told him I was driving you home and he got . . . pissy."

"Why?"

"Because he wants to do it," Jakes said. "Come on, let's go. My car's out front."

# Chapter 36

I assumed the car we were in was Jakes's own. It was a Toyota, and looked too new and clean to be a police car; besides, there was no radio in it. In fact, Julia eventually asked him about that.

"We do a lot of communications with cell phones now," he told her, "although we have portable radios, as well. But we usually do drive a department car. We were actually going off duty when this call came in."

After that, Julia, relegated to the backseat, fell silent.

"I don't see anything in this car to indicate children," I said. "Does your wife have her own car?"

"I don't have a wife or kids, Alex. That's my partner, remember?"

I was trying to make conversation, and didn't want to talk in front of Julia about her mother and father being murdered. I also found myself a little curious about his status.

"Why haven't you ever gotten married?"

"Oh, I've been married," he said. "Twice. I'm the biggest cliché in the department, the cop so married to his job he can't keep a wife happy."

"Is that true?"

"Why else would they both have cheated on me?"

"Maybe it was a failing in them," I said. "Did you ever consider that?"

He looked at me quickly, then back at the road.

"Actually, yeah, I did think that once," he said, "but I thought I was just being an asshole."

"Maybe you like being as asshole," I said.

"Well, I've pretty much been one to you, haven't I?" he asked.

"I suppose that's the way you do your job," I said. "Annoy the hell out of your suspects until they confess."

"Touché."

Sure enough, when we got to my house there wasn't a reporter or camera in sight, but I suddenly had second thoughts about being there, anyway. About having Julia, Sarah and my mom there, as well.

"Don't worry," Jakes said, as if reading my mind, "I'm going to have someone watching the house."

"Yeah, but for how long?"

"Until we catch the killer," he promised.

He walked us inside and asked where my mother and Sarah were.

"She has a place out back by the canal."

"It might be better for all of you to stay in the same house."

"We're not going to stay locked up," I said. "I have to go out—"

"I can't have a man cover you if you go out, Alex," he warned.

"Whoever the killer is, they're not going to try to kill me out in public. I think they've already proven that."

"We don't know how desperate this killer is going to get," Jakes said. "Now he's killed two people and tried for you. He—or she—is escalating."

"I'll be careful when I go out."

"Maybe you can have your boyfriend go with you," he suggested.

"I can take care of myself," I said. "Besides, we kind of had a fight. . . ."

"Oh? About what?"

I looked at him to see if he was being cute.

"Never mind."

"Hey, Julia," he called, turning toward her. "You've been real quiet. How about a hug goodbye?"

Julia fell into his arms and he hugged her tightly while she held on to him. It must have felt nice. I was wondering what I'd do if he offered me a hug.

Then I wondered how I'd feel if he didn't.

I walked Jakes out to his car after telling Julia to make herself at home.

"I hope she won't be much trouble," he said, "but this has to be better than putting her in a women's shelter. I mean, she's still a child."

Jakes's concern for Julia's well-being had me looking at him in a whole different light. I guess I'd been seeing him all along as a cop, and not as an attractive single man.

Down girl, you've got a guy—or do you?

"She'll be fine," I said. "Maybe she and Sarah will get along. Neither of them has a sister. They might like it."

"You've got a point," he said. "I hope it works out. I'll be, uh, checking in on her, if that's okay."

"That's fine."

"In fact, I'd better just check in on the whole family." He reached into his pocket, took out a card; then he took my hand and pressed the card into my palm.

"All my numbers are on there, including my cell," he said. "Call me if you need anything, or if you even think anything is wrong."

"Um, you said something about having someone watch," I said, lamely.

"Right across the street, that black Crown Victoria," he said. "That's one of my men. He'll be relieved by someone else with the same car."

"Should we invite him in? I mean, give him coffee or anything?"

"He'll be fine just where he is," Jakes said. "I'll pull up alongside and speak to him before I leave."

He was still holding on to my hand, and it wasn't that I minded as much as it made me self-conscious. I eased mine from his as gently as I could.

"I—we all appreciate this, Detective."

"It's my job, Alex," he told me.

"It's more than a job with you, isn't it, Detective?"

"Frank," he said, "my first name is Frank, and yes, it is more than a job with me. I'm glad you noticed."

With that he turned and walked to his car. As promised, he swung it around until it was parallel with his man's car. They had a conversation, and then Jakes drove away. I looked down at his business card. It was funny, but I thought I could still feel the pressure of his hand.

I turned and went into the house.

# Chapter 37

Julia and Sarah took to each other immediately, which was a relief. In no time Julia was chasing Sarah around the house, and my mother was watching them, already fond of her newly acquired granddaughter.

Which was good, because she was going to be stuck with them the next day.

Paul had said I was out of it because Jakes no longer counted me as a suspect. I thought that was remarkably shortsighted of him. After all, someone had killed a coworker of mine and had apparently meant for me to take the blame. Then when I wouldn't sit still for that, they tried to kill me and make it look like suicide.

It was all very frightening, I admit, and I probably should have just hidden in the house with Jakes's man outside watching us. But I couldn't do it. I was too mad and—okay—carried away with my role as amateur detective—even if I hadn't been a very good one up to now. But out of it? I didn't think so.

I couldn't remember who'd said it to me in the hospital—or maybe I'd just thought of it myself—but someone I had already interviewed may have tried to kill me or have me killed. I intended to retrace my steps and talk to all the same people. Was I frightened? You bet, but even more than that, I was mad. Suppose Sarah had been with me when I pulled my car into the garage? What would the killer have done? Put her in the car next to me? Just the thought of that made me furious. It also made me want to hug the stuffing out of Sarah, so I joined Julia in chasing her, and in no time we were passing her back and forth, and she was giggling like crazy.

But while we were getting along, we were also very nervous. The last twenty-four hours had brought us all some sort of trauma, and we were jumping at shadows and flinching every time a floorboard creaked, even with the police presence outside.

"You know," my mother said to me at one point, "I've seen plenty of movies where they leave one cop outside and he ends up sitting behind the wheel of his car—dead. And nobody knows it until too late."

We were in the kitchen. Julia and Sarah were watching TV, and my mother was keeping her voice down.

"Mom, if you think he's dead, take him a cup of coffee and check."

"I'm not going out there," she said. "Something could happen between here and his car. And why's he parked across the street?"

Suddenly, Julia and Sarah were in the kitchen with us.

"What's wrong?" I asked.

"Nothing," Julia said.

My daughter was much more truthful.

"We heard a noise outside."

"You see?" my mother whispered. "Somebody could be coming from the canals."

"Why don't we ask the policeman in the car across the street to come and have some milk?" Sarah asked.

I stared at her. I didn't even think she was aware of the cop across the street.

"That's it," I said. "Everybody pack a bag. Julia, I have some clothes that will fit you until we can get your stuff. Or else we'll go out and buy some new stuff."

"Shopping?" she asked. Even traumatized teenage girls respond to shopping.

"Sure, why not? Shopping. But first I'm going to go and talk to the nice policeman across the street."

"Where are we going?" Sarah asked.

"It's a surprise."

I headed for the front door.

"Check and see if he's dead," my mother hissed at me.

He wasn't dead.

Twenty minutes later we were all in my kid car and the nice policeman was following us. I'd told him that we were too nervous to stay in the house, since somebody had already tried to kill me there.

"I can't say I blame you, ma'am," the detective had said.

It was a nice thing to say, but God, I hated to be called "ma'am"! Especially by a man who was at least ten years older than I was. I piled everyone into the car and we drove to Silverlake.

"Whose house are we going to?" Sarah asked.

"My friend George," I told her. And then to Julia I said, "He does my hair on the show. He lives in a beautiful 1920s Spanish with his partner. Lots of room."

I'd called George on my cell and he'd invited us all over, even though I had sort of already done that myself.

When we got there Wayne had the door open and was waiting for us.

"You poor things," he said, giving me a loving and remarkably powerful hug for such a slender man, and then quickly hugging Sarah, who returned it in kind. "Come in, come in. I'm Wayne. You must be Alex's mother. I can see where she gets her looks from. Come in, darling," he said to Julia. "You'll be safe here—and comfortable. George, they're here!"

"I know they're here," George said, greeting us in the living room. "I can hear you chattering."

He also gave Sarah and me a hug, and extended his hands to my mother and Julia, squeezing theirs reassuringly.

"You're all welcome to stay as long as you want. We have two guest rooms. You can split them up any way you like."

"I want to stay with Julia!" Sarah shouted.

"If it's all right with Julia, and your mom, that's what you'll do," George told her.

"It's fine with me," Julia told me.

"Okay, then I'll room with Mom."

"And we'll have dinner—I hope you haven't eaten yet?" Wayne asked.

"I'm hungry!" Sarah chimed in.

"Good, we'll eat dinner, and then we'll make some s'mores."

"Yay!" Sarah yelled.

George and Wayne were great. They were treating it as one big pajama party/sleepover. Meanwhile, there was still a cop outside the door in case somebody tried to kill me—again.

# Chapter 38

It was a big party until Sarah's eyes finally started to close. Luckily, Julia was also pretty wiped out, so when I announced it was time for Sarah to go to bed and she protested, even with her eyes at half-mast, Julia announced, "Me, too," and that solved that problem. I mouthed a silent "Thank you" to her as she marched Sarah off to their room.

"I think I'm going to turn in, too," my mother said. "The last couple of days have just been too exciting for me."

"Good night, Mom," I said.

I wondered about my mother and how she'd stand up to this. So far she'd just been too quiet and too calm. I knew I'd been neglecting my family in the face of these murders. I wondered how cops managed to juggle business and home life—then remembered what Jakes said about being divorced, and figured they didn't do it very well.

When it was just me and George sitting in their tasteful, artistically furnished living room, Wayne came in carrying two glasses of white wine.

"You two probably want to talk," he said, "so I'll

say good night. I'll be up early to make breakfast for everyone."

"You don't have to do that, Wayne—"

"Hush," he said. "I never get a chance to make a big breakfast. This one's always running late and just wants coffee and a muffin."

"Leave him alone," George told me. "He's in his element now, entertaining."

"You help this diva solve all her problems, Georgie," Wayne said, giving his partner a kiss good night. "Girl, you are the only reason I watch that show of yours."

I opened up my mouth to protest the diva reference, then just gave up. Obviously, it comes with the territory.

"He's a gem," I said. "Don't you let him get away."

"I have no intention of doing that," George said.

They were a great couple. Together for so long and really kind to each other. Their union was my model for a healthy relationship. Two gay guys. Why not?

Georgie got up and plopped down right next to me. "Okay, let's hear it—I mean really hear it. I've read the tabloids, but I need to get the real stuff from you. Tell me everything that's been going on."

So I did, starting with somebody trying to gas me. . . .

"You poor thing," George said, when I finished, "but everything's all right now, isn't it? I mean, you're not a suspect anymore."

"There is that," I said, "but someone still tried to kill me, George."

"Yes, but if you stop asking questions, why would they try again?"

Essentially, he was telling me the same thing Paul had, to back off. Which reminded me. Had I treated Paul badly at the Roswell house? I had to call him.

"I can't do that, George."

"Why?"

"Truthfully?" I put down my wineglass and pulled my knees up to my chest. "This all scares the hell out of me, George . . . and I've never felt more alive. I have to see this through to the end or I won't be able to live with myself. I know I've been stumbling around, but you know what? I'm also so damn mad. And when I get mad, I get stubborn. Any of that make sense?"

"All of it, I guess."

"Then there's Julia," I said. "She was kind of a brat to me when I first met her, but she's not a bad kid, and she's alone."

"Why would anyone want to kill that sweet child?" he asked.

"Why did anyone want to kill her parents?" I countered.

"Well, Marcy was a bitch," George said.

"And her ex-husband?"

"What did he do for a living?"

"He was a businessman," I said. "An investor, I think."

"There you go," George said. "He made deals. He probably cheated somebody. Maybe his murder and hers aren't related."

"That would be a heck of a coincidence, wouldn't it?" I asked.

"Well, it could be true," George said. "We know one thing for sure."

"What's that?"

"The attempt on you has nothing to do with his murder," George said. "He wasn't even dead yet when you started your investigation."

"So I still only have to be concerned with hers, even though the cops probably think the killer is the same."

We were sitting at opposite ends of the sofa, facing each other, each leaning an elbow of one arm on the back while holding a glass of wine in the other. And we were clicking, sort of playing dueling motives and theories.

"You should be leaving both to the police," he said, "but at least you can leave his."

"I feel bad for her," I said, "for Julia . . . and for Marcy. Divorced, fending for herself . . . I identify with her a little, although I can't imagine ever denying my child."

"You have enough to do with feeling bad for yourself," George said. "If you're going to do this and keep doing it right, you're going to have to concentrate."

I nodded. "Starting tomorrow I'll retrace my steps, talk to the same people, see who looks nervous—"

"See who tries to kill you again?"

"I hope not," I said.

We both sipped wine and I saw his eyes starting to droop. I wondered if he could notice mine doing the same thing. So tired we were both being wiped out by one glass of wine.

"You know, there's one thing I wanted to do that I never did."

"What's that?"

"Go to Marcy's house."

"Didn't she live in the Hollywood Hills somewhere?"

"Yes," I said, "I was there once for a cast party when she got the job."

"What do you expect to find there?"

"I don't know," I said. "But I do know I want to have a look."

"How will you get in?"

"I'll improvise."

"Well, I'm going to improvise myself into bed right now," he said. "You can use the guest bath. We won't hear a thing. We're on the other side of the house."

"Okay," I said. "Give me your glass."

He did so, and then leaned down and kissed me on the cheek.

"You and your crew can stay as long as you like."

"You're the best, George."

"I know it," he said. "Good night."

While he went off to bed, I took the two wineglasses to the kitchen and rinsed them out. Then I fished out my cell phone to call Paul, but it vibrated at that moment. I checked the readout and saw it was him.

"I'm sorry," I said. "I was just about to call you to apolo—"

"Alex, don't," he said. "I acted like an ass and I'm sorry."

Basically we did a kiss-and-make-up session on the phone, and then I invited him to breakfast the next morning. We said good night, and I was oddly pleased that he hadn't said, "I love you."

I walked to the front of the house and looked out the window to make sure our cop was still there.

"Why *do* you park on the other side of the street?" I wondered aloud.

I was going to have to ask Jakes if that was some sort of procedure.

I stood there until I saw a small flare in the car. He was lighting a cigarette. Satisfied that he was, indeed, still alive, I went to bed.

# Chapter 39

True to his word we all woke up to delicious smells coming from the kitchen as Wayne whipped up a huge breakfast for us all. When I got out there George was helping him, and they even had Sarah happily mixing pancake batter. And sitting at the table with a cup of coffee was Paul.

"He was parked on the doorstep when I got up," Wayne said, "so I took pity."

Paul kissed me and I gave him a big hug.

"Hi, Mommy," Sarah called out.

"Good morning, baby," I said. I could hear the bacon sizzling and smell it cooking; the aroma of strong coffee also filled the room.

"Mom is still asleep," I said.

"So's Julia. She snores," Sarah said. "It's funny."

I figured she wouldn't think snoring was fun when she grew up, got married and found out her husband did it.

"George snores, too," Wayne said.

"I do not."

Wayne turned from the stove and stuck his tongue out at him.

"I breathe heavily, darling," George told Sarah. "It's not the same thing at all."

Sarah giggled.

"I like it here, Mommy," she said. "Everybody's funny."

Thank God she thought it was all fun and games.

"Can I help?" I asked.

"Yes," Wayne said, handing me a mug of coffee, "take this and get out of my kitchen. And you'll have to be the bad guys and wake the other ladies when it's time to eat, because we're having only one sitting this morning."

"Gotcha."

I walked to the front window and looked out. The car was still there. A man was in it, but I had no idea if it was the same man or not. I was tempted to take him some coffee, but Jakes had said not to.

I considered my options for the day and decided to stick with my plan. I was going to go to Marcy's house and have a look around. I just didn't know if the policeman would follow, or stay here to watch over Julia. Which of us was the priority? I wondered.

"Time!" Wayne called out.

I went and woke Momma first, then went along to the room Julia was sharing with Sarah. From the hall I could hear that Sarah was right. Julia did snore—like a buzz saw.

"Julia, honey?" I called softly. I wasn't prepared for her reaction. She came out of her deep sleep with her eyes wide, sat straight up and was about to scream. I put the coffee mug down and grabbed her, held her

tightly and told her everything was okay; she was safe.
I stroked her hair until she calmed down.

"I—I forgot where I was," she finally said.

"I know," I said. "I did that myself this morning
when I woke up. Are you all right now?"

"Y-yes." She leaned back. "Is—is that bacon I smell?
I'm a vegetarian. Now I really want to puke!"

"It's not just meat by-products. I'm sure we can rus-
tle you up something on the veggie side," I said, "and
Wayne wants everybody out there now."

She was wearing a T-shirt and a pair of panties.

"I—I'll put on some shorts, wash my face and be
right out."

"Okay, sweetheart."

"Nobody's ever called me that," she said, as I stood
up and grabbed my mug.

"What?"

"Sweetheart," she said. "I don't remember my
mother calling me anything but Julia, and my dad—
well, he called me his princess."

"Would you like me to stop calling you that?" I
asked. "I'm sorry, it's something I call Sarah. It just
comes out."

"No, no," she said, kind of embarrassed, "I like it.
It's fine."

"Okay, then," I said. "I'll see you at the table. You
better make it quick. Everybody's starving."

"Thank you, Alex," she said. "For everything. I was
such a . . . bitch when we first met."

"You were no such thing. Well okay, you were, but I
understand," I said.

I went out to the dining room, where the table was

set with bowls of scrambled eggs, plates of bacon, a platter of pancakes, lots of toast, more coffee, and Wayne had even made tea for my mother. There was even a plate of cut-up fresh fruit.

"This is amazing, Wayne," my mother said. "Thank you so much."

"Now you see why I keep him around," George said.

Julia came out looking freshly scrubbed, still wearing her T-shirt and a pair of cutoff jeans.

"Wow," she said, when she saw the table.

"I wanna sit next to Julia," Sarah yelled.

"Come on, then, half-pint," Julia said.

We all got seated and started passing the bowls and platters around. Paul sat on Sarah's other side so he could poke her from time to time, and across from me.

"No diets this morning," Wayne said, smiling, "for any of us."

George was sitting next to me. He leaned over and asked, "Are you still going to Marcy's house today?"

"Yes."

"What about your bodyguard?"

"I have a feeling he's Julia's bodyguard," I said. "We'll see."

"What's this about going to Marcy's?" Paul asked.

"I'll tell you after breakfast," I promised.

We devoured the breakfast Wayne had laid out, and then helped clear the table and take everything into the kitchen.

"What are we supposed to do with ourselves now, honey?" my mother asked, coming up next to me.

"You're going to stay here with Wayne and George, Mom, and watch out for Julia and Sarah."

"And you?"

"I have to go out."

My mother sighed.

"Why does that not surprise me?"

Later when I was getting ready to leave I explained to Paul what I was going to do.

"Let me call the studio," he said. "I'm supposed to work today, but I can reschedule the scenes—"

"You don't have to do that," I said. "I'm only going to look at an empty house."

"You mean you're going to break into an empty house. Alex, you can't—"

"Paul, I don't know how to break into a house," I said. "I just . . . feel a need to go there and snoop around a little."

"All right," he said, "I'm not going to argue with you. You want to do this on your own, but you know I'm only a cell phone call away, okay? You call and I'll come running."

"I know you will."

He drew me into his arms and kissed me, and I kissed him back for a while.

"So we're okay?" he asked.

I kissed him again, and said, "We're very okay." But I had this annoying feeling that I wasn't being one hundred percent honest.

# Chapter 40

By the time I was ready to leave, my mother, Julia and Sarah were already outside by the pool with George and Wayne. I got five waves good-bye and George called out for me to be careful.

I went out the front door and happily noted there were no photographers. I crossed the street to the cop in the car. He sat up straight as he saw me coming and put a container of coffee on the dashboard. He looked impossibly young for his job.

"Good morning, Detective," I said.

"Officer, ma'am," he said. "Just Officer, uh, Bailey."

I winced at the "ma'am." "Okay, Officer Bailey, I have to go and run some errands."

"Really?" He looked concerned. "Ma'am, my orders are to stay with the younger wom—I mean, the teenage, uh, the one named Julia?"

"That's fine," I said. "I won't be out long, and since my mother and daughter are also in the house, I'll feel better if you stay here."

"I'm, uh, also supposed to radio in to Detective Jakes if you leave the premises."

"That's fine," I said. "I wouldn't want you to get into trouble for not doing your job."

"Uh, thank you, ma'am. Could you wait while I, uh, ma'am—"

"Would you mind not calling me "ma'am"? It's just a thing I have. . . ."

"Oh, I'm so sorry, ma'am. I mean miss." Okay, so that didn't sound right, either.

He was scrambling for his radio as I walked away from his car, got into mine and drove away.

I probably should have been too afraid to come out of the house after someone had tried to kill me, but as I told George, mostly I was still mad. I didn't see anybody following me, so I felt pretty safe, and my family was surrounded by men.

There was no chance that the killer would be waiting there for me. Why would he be? And if he just happened to be there—well, that was too much of a coincidence to even consider, wasn't it?

So, to my way of thinking I was completely safe driving to Marcy's house in Hollywood Hills.

I pulled up in front of Marcy's house and got out of my car, looking around for murderers and, even worse, photographers. When none leaped out of the bushes I walked up to the front door. When I reached it I felt silly. What was I planning to do, ring the bell? I tried the doorknob; naturally it was locked. I turned, stood on the doorstep and looked around. I had to drive up a winding driveway to reach the house. There was a gate, but it had been opened. From where I stood I could not see any neighbors' homes, and I assumed the neighbors could not see me.

I decided to take a walk around the house and see if I could find an open door or window. It didn't take long. When I got to the north side of the house, there was a pair of French doors that stood ajar. The glass wasn't broken. It looked as if someone had simply left them open. I stood back and inspected them. Again I thought what were the odds that someone was actually in there at exactly the same time?

This is the part in the movie theater where you want to yell at the heroine, "No, no, don't go in there!" and she goes in anyway. That moment could never be adequately explained to film critics—"Thumbs-down because having her go into the house at that moment just didn't make sense to me, Roger"—but in I went. Later I'd be asked to explain why I did.

I found myself in a dining room, complete with table, chairs and hutch. They were horrible. I'd always noticed Marcy's terrible taste in clothes, and it seemed to have carried over to her home furnishings. It appeared to be 1970s style. But not good 1970s. If there is such a thing. Ugly colonial furniture and lots of *chachkis*. You know, glass birds, porcelain angels with dried flowers glued on. All she was missing were a few velvet paintings. I was trying to give her the benefit of the doubt. Maybe all this crap had sentimental value to her. And then I remembered whom I was thinking about. Not a sentimental bone in her dead body.

I moved slowly through the house, looking for

signs of somebody else being there. I was halfway down a hallway when I heard it.

There *was* someone else in the house.

Somebody was moving around, and not doing it quietly. I started to look around for a place to hide. Then I decided to retrace my steps to the French doors and get out of there. I turned, went back down the hallway and tripped over a god-awful brass umbrella stand. The stand hit the hutch and knocked over the glass bird. *Crash!* I heard movement from the other end of the hall.

Somebody was coming.

I sprinted for the French doors, but Marcy had this ugly two-tone braided rug on the floor that slid out from under my feet after I'd taken only two steps. I went down on my tailbone—hard.

The woman was dead and her furnishings were trying to get me killed, too. I struggled to get to my feet. My butt and my pride were hurting, and then something hit me on the head and all the hurt faded away. . . .

# Chapter 41

When I came to, Jakes was kneeling next to me, looking down at me. God, he was cute, and he smelled good, too. Paul smelled good, but different. Flustered, I started to sit up, but my head and his hand stopped me.

"Take it easy, Alex," he said. "You got hit on the head—again. I swear, you're worse than a fictional private eye."

He pushed me back to the floor, and I realized he was in shirtsleeves, and his jacket was folded and slipped beneath my head.

"Wha-what happened?" I asked.

"You remember where you are?"

"Marcy's house."

"Apparently you walked in on somebody," he said. "They knocked you out and took off."

"Somebody?" I asked. "It wasn't the killer?"

"If it was," Jakes said, "I think you'd be dead right now."

"How did you get here?" he asked.

"My man radioed me that you left the house," he said. "I called and talked to your friend George. He told me where you went. When I got here I found the doors wide-open and you out cold on the floor."

"I—when I got here those doors were already open." It seemed important for me to tell him that.

"Don't worry," he said. "I'm not going to run you in for breaking and entering."

"Good," I said, "I thought—"

"I might run you in for being stupid, though," he added.

"I didn't—" I tried to sit up, but he stopped me again.

"I know," he said, "you had to do it. What did you think you'd find here?"

"I don't know," I said, "but I certainly wouldn't find anything by just staying home."

"You wouldn't have another bump on your head if you had," he said. "Here, let me have a look. Sit up."

Now he wanted me to sit up! He took my hand and helped me, then put his hands to the back of my head. I was very conscious of several things—the touch of his fingers, the smell of his cologne and the closeness of his body.

"I'm fine," I said, flinching.

"It's right near the other bump," he said. "You might have a concussion."

"I'm not going back to that hospital," I said, swatting his hands away. "Just help me up."

"Okay, but let's go slow, and if you feel dizzy, grab on to me."

Yeah, maybe not such a bad idea.

"Are you all right?" he asked when I was on my feet.

"Fine," I said. "I'm going to need some Tylenol or aspirin, but I'm fine."

"I didn't call for paramedics, but I could—"

"No," I said, "there's no need. So . . . did I walk in on a burglary?"

"Probably," he said. "It happens with some of these homes where people live alone. Once the obituary runs, the house becomes a target."

"Why'd they wait so long?" I asked.

"Maybe they weren't the first ones," he suggested. "Maybe somebody saw the open door, like you did, and decided it was too good to pass up."

I looked around. The house was kind of neat for a place that had been burglarized more than once.

"Since we're here, I'd still like to take a look at her office."

"Why?" he asked. "Len and I have been through it. Lab people have been through it."

"Where's all the yellow tape?"

"No tape," he said. "This was never a crime scene. We simply went through it because it was the victim's home."

"Well, maybe I'll see something in her office that you missed."

"If I don't let you do it, are you just gonna sneak back here later?"

"Probably," I said. "I'd hate to think I got hit on the head for nothing."

He studied me for a moment. I thought he had something he wanted to tell me, but then he said, "Okay, a quick look, and then we're out of here."

"Agreed," I said. "Where's the office?"

"Back here."

He led the way back to the hall I'd gotten halfway down. At the far end was a doorway, which led to a small office. I was surprised. It was furnished in a very businesslike fashion, with none of the horrible taste exhibited throughout the rest of the house.

The desk and file cabinets were inexpensive stuff you could pretty much get in any Office Max.

"Looks like nothing's been touched," I said.

"Cops only trash places in the movies," he said. "We were pretty thorough."

There was nothing on the walls, no pictures or plaques, nothing to indicate that the person who worked here was in television.

"I know," he said, reading my mind. "Looks like she kept all her memorabilia and awards in her office."

"Can I touch—"

"This is not a crime scene," he said. "But make it quick. I've got something to do, and something to tell you."

"What?"

"Finish here first," he said.

I went to the desk, opened the drawers, moved stuff around. She was neat. Most people have a drawer that they keep sweeping stuff into from their desktop, but she apparently wasn't in that habit. After the desk I moved to the file cabinets, opening and closing them. I wasn't finding anything helpful, but would I have recognized it if I had?

I was starting to feel foolish.

"What is it you want to tell me?" I asked.

"You done here?"

"I suppose," I said. "I really don't—okay." I flapped my arms. "I'm wasting your time. You have somewhere to go."

He looked at his watch and said, "Well, I did. I'll just have to go back to Parker Center now. They'll already have him in custody by now."

"What? Who's in custody? For what?"

"Len and I were on our way to make an arrest, Alex, when I got this call."

"You came here instead of making your arrest?"

"I was worried about you," he said. "Len took some uniforms with him and did the honors."

"Are you saying you arrested the man who killed Marcy?"

"Yes."

"Who is it? Jesus, why didn't you tell me this right away?"

"I was going to—look, this is not easy. I know you're friends. I didn't want to blurt it out, and I wasn't sure what kind of shape you were in after being hit on the head again—"

"Go ahead," I said, "be my guest. When you're arresting somebody's friend, you're entitled to blurt away."

"It's one of the actors from your soap," he said. "Andy McIntyre."

# Chapter 42

"He has a life coach, for Chrissake. He doesn't take a pee without checking with him first," I said.

I insisted on going to Parker Center with Jakes. He said I would have to leave my car and ride with him.

"That doesn't mean he's not a murderer."

"What possible motive—"

"Come on, Alex," Jakes said. "A lot of you on the show had a motive. Ever since she took over, some parts changed, some got smaller."

Mine was one of those that changed. Andy's had gotten smaller, but did that mean he'd kill because of it? I didn't think so, knowing Andy the way I did.

"This is ridiculous," I said. "It can't be Andy."

"Well, we'll find out for sure when we get there," Jakes said. "They've got instructions to wait for me before interrogating him."

"What about a lawyer?"

"That's his business," Jakes said. "Maybe he'll have his life coach get him one."

He said Andy was a strong suspect all along—even stronger than me—because although I'd had a loud argument with her at work, he'd had a public one some days earlier out in the parking lot.

"How can that be?" I asked. "I never heard anything about it."

"We questioned everyone who works at the studio," he said, "including maintenance staff. One of them saw Andy and Marcy having a violent argument."

"Violent?"

"He pushed her."

"Andy? If he put his hands on Marcy, she drove him to it."

"And drove him to murder, apparently."

"Andy was on the set with the rest of us when the light fell, while Marcy was being killed."

"No, he wasn't," Jakes said. "Nobody remembers actually seeing him there after the light fell." He turned his head and looked at me. "Do you?"

I tried to go back six days in my head, but it was no use.

"No," I admitted.

"Then he has no alibi, and he has a motive. But we have the blood trail."

"Wait a minute," I said. "That's the trail from Henry Roswell's house? You mean to tell me you're arresting him for both murders?"

According to Jakes they had followed a blood trail—just a few drops, starting with the one I had found on the tiles yesterday outside Henry Roswell's house—leading down the beach to Andy's house.

He hesitated a moment, then said, "We're arresting him on suspicion of double homicide."

"Why would he kill her ex-husband?"

"That's what he's going to tell us," Jakes assured me.

When we got to Parker Center the press was there in full force. Jakes drove through the crowd slowly and we entered the parking structure beneath the building.

As we got out of the car he said, "Alex, this is a courtesy from me to you. You have to keep quiet when we go inside."

"I want to watch you interrogate him," I said.

"I can't let you—"

"Come on," I said, "you're going to put him in a room with a one-way mirror, aren't you? I know him better than you do. Let me watch. I may be able to help. You know, watch his body language? You hire people to do that all the time, right? Consultants?"

He stared at me across the top of the car, drumming his fingers.

"I should've made you go home."

"But you didn't and it's too late now," I said. "So use me. I won't get in the way. Promise."

"All right, come on."

We went to an elevator and I didn't even notice on which floor we got off. I followed him down a hallway crowded with people walking in both directions. Some of them were going where we were going, so we followed them in.

"Here he is," Detective Davis said.

"Jakes, what the fuck—," a large, florid-faced man with white hair started to say, but he stopped short when he saw me.

"She'd better not be a reporter you promised to give an exclusive to," he told Jakes.

"She's not, Chief," he said. "This is Alexis Peterson. She's one of the stars on *The Yearning Tide*. Alex, this is Chief of Detectives Pierce."

I could see Pierce wanted to tear into Jakes, but he was holding back on my account.

"Jakes, could we have Ms. Peterson taken to a waiting room until—"

"I need her here, Chief."

"What for?" the big man asked impatiently.

"She knows the suspect better than anyone," Jakes said. "I want her to sit in on the interrogation as a . . . consultant."

"A consultant?" Pierce asked. If looks could kill Jakes would have been dead on the spot.

"Yes, a . . . soap opera consultant."

That sounded so ludicrous even to me that I knew I owed Jakes big for this.

"Chief, I don't believe Mr. McIntyre is capable of one murder, let alone two."

"Ms. Peterson," the chief said, with exaggerated politeness, "while I would bow to your superior knowledge of soap operas, I don't believe your expertise in police work—"

"Chief, can we get on with the interrogation?" Jakes asked. "With all due respect, this is still my case and I'm entitled to bring in a consultant."

I saw the muscles in the chief's jaw moving before he spoke. I wondered how many molars he'd just ground down.

"Len, is he in the room?" Jakes asked.

"Yep." Davis had been watching the entire three-way exchange with an amused expression on his face.

"Then can we get to it?" Jakes asked.

I wasn't sure whom he was asking, but the chief finally said, "All right, let's do it."

# Chapter 43

Standing next to the chief of detectives, both of us staring through the two-way mirror at a shaking, pale Andy McIntyre and his attorney (I didn't know if the studio had sent the man, or if Andy's life coach had called him), I could feel the chief's disapproval of my being there.

Jakes started asking Andy questions about Marcy cutting his part, about how his career was winding down and how she was making it worse. Andy kept saying he didn't kill Marcy, he couldn't kill anyone, but Jakes kept at him. Why did Andy have to kill Marcy's ex-husband? Had the man found out what Andy did? Threaten to call the police? And would he have killed the daughter, too, if he'd found her hiding in the house? Andy kept nervously brushing his hair away from his eyes, or leaning over to whisper into his attorney's ear. I saw he was close to tears. I felt so sorry for him.

Perversely—for I knew he'd hate it if I spoke—I said to the chief, "He didn't do it."

"Really?"

"Look at him," I said. "He's so scared he can't sit still."

"I hate to disappoint you, Ms. Peterson," the chief said, pointing with a big sausagelike finger, "but that's how guilty men look."

Andy was sweating so much his collar looked wet.

"That may be so," I said, "but that's also the look of a man having a heart attack. You're scaring poor Andy to death."

"Ms. Peterson—"

"And where's his life coach?" I said.

"The what?"

"He doesn't go anywhere without Murray the Life Coach."

"Ms. Peterson," he said, turning his head to look at me, "this is serious business—"

"So is this," I said, pointing into the room. "He's a sick man, Chief."

"I don't see—," the chief said, but then he looked back into the room and saw what I saw.

Jakes was rushing around the table to catch Andy when he fell out of his chair. The lawyer leaped out of his chair and backed away, as if Andy were contagious. Jakes turned to look at us and started waving, then pulled out his cell phone and dialed three digits.

"Get in there!" the chief shouted to Detective Davis.

"Yes, sir!"

"And get an ambulance!" he snapped. "The last thing we need is our prime suspect dying of a heart attack while in custody."

I felt so bad for Andy, but there was nothing I could do.

"You know this man so well," the chief said accusingly. "You couldn't tell us he had a bad heart?"

"He doesn't have a bad heart that I know of," I said, "but I told you that you were scaring him to death."

He turned to face me and I thought he was going to let me have it. His face turned red; I wondered if he was having a stroke. Wouldn't that be some coincidence? But then he stormed past me and out of the room. I saw Davis enter the interview room to help Jakes with Andy, who was now lying on his back. The lawyer had pressed his back to the wall and was staring. They'd brought Andy in wearing a jogging suit, so there was really no collar to loosen. I could see they were talking to him, trying to make him as comfortable as they could.

The chief didn't enter the room, so I assumed he had hightailed it to his office to try and work out some sort of statement for the press.

Jakes turned again, looked at me and waved. At least, I thought he was waving at me, telling me to come into the room. Since I was alone that made sense, so I left and went down the hall to enter the interview room.

"Talk to him, Alex," Jakes said. "We have an ambulance coming, and I want to keep him calm."

"First you scare him out of his wits and now you want to keep him calm?" I asked, but I got on my knees next to Andy and grabbed his hand.

"Alex?"

"You're going to be all right, Andy."

I looked at Jakes.

"Could be a heart attack," Jakes said, "or it might be

an anxiety attack. We'll know more when the EMTs get here."

Andy squeezed my hand.

"Murray," he said, "where's Murray?"

"Who's Murray?" Jakes asked.

"His life coach."

"His what?"

"There was another man at the house when we picked him up," Davis said, "but we wouldn't take him along."

"I'm surprised he didn't follow you," I said.

"He might have trouble getting into the building," Davis said.

"Alex—"

"I'm here, Andy," I said, holding his hand in both of mine. "Stay calm. You're going to be fine."

"I didn't kill Marcy, Alex," he said. "I didn't kill anyone."

His eyes were closed, his lids fluttering, but he continued to drone on about how he hadn't killed anyone.

"I know, Andy, I know . . . ," I assured him, saying the only words I could think of.

I hoped Jakes was right, and that it could have been an anxiety attack, because to me Andy looked gray. His palm was sweaty. . . . He looked really bad. . . .

# Chapter 44

I went to the hospital with Jakes and from the waiting room called George's house to let everyone know what was going on.

"Are they crazy?" George asked. "That man couldn't kill anyone."

"That's what I told them, but it didn't carry much weight."

"I have a question."

"What?"

"Are we going to work tomorrow?"

"You are," I said. "I don't know about me." As for Wayne, he was a writer and he worked at home. "I'll have to wait and see. I might have to give Thomas a call in the morning and explain my situation. If there's a murderer after me, I don't think he'd want me to bring him to the set."

"I think the whole production company would appreciate it if you didn't," George agreed.

"Okay, I've got to go. Here comes a doctor."

"Tell Andy—," he started, but I cut him off.

Jakes saw the doctor at the same time I did and we all met in the center of the waiting room.

"Is there a family member here?" the doctor asked.

"This man is under arrest, Doctor," Jakes said. "Ms. Peterson, here, is the closest to a family member we've got."

The doctor was young and had an earnest expression permanently placed on his face, probably hoping patients would take him seriously. He looked at me and said, "You're on TV, right?"

"Doctor?"

"Sorry, Mr. McIntyre has suffered a mild heart attack. I'd almost call it an anxiety attack, but there is slight damage."

"When can I take him out of here?" Jakes asked.

"Oh, not until tomorrow, I'm afraid, and maybe not even then. I want to watch him tonight, and reevaluate in the morning."

"What's your name?" Jakes asked.

"Dr. Steinberg."

"Thank you, Doctor. I'll be looking for you in the morning."

"I'll be here," Steinberg said. "I just came on duty."

He turned to leave, then stopped and looked at me again.

"You are on TV, right?"

"Yes, I'm afraid I am."

"Sorry," he said, "I just moved here from the Midwest. Not used to seeing celebrities, yet."

"You'll get sick of 'em," Jakes said. "They're all over the place."

I stared at Jakes as the doctor walked away and he said, "Well, you are."

"I am?"

"You people," Jakes said. "Celebrities."

"You're not making any points here, Detective," I said. "What are you going to do about Andy?"

"I'll keep a man here overnight to watch him," he said. "I'll be back first thing in the morning to take him back to Parker Center."

"And put him back in that room?" I asked. "You'll be right back here in no time."

"I doubt I'll be able to put him in that room again without his lawyer's okay, after this," he said. "He'll probably have a doctor advise against it."

"The studio will probably step in, too," I said, "to try to keep him safe."

"Would they do that for you?"

"I hope so."

"You know, I shouldn't tell you this," he said, "but I like you, so I will."

"I'm flattered."

"Those people you work with, they were all so quick to believe you might've done it, might've killed Marcy Blanchard. A couple of them even went so far as to say maybe you had."

"I know," I said. "I found that out myself."

"How can you work with those people?"

"Up to now I haven't had a problem," I said. "But after this . . ."

I let it trail off. Now wasn't the time for me to wonder about my future on the show. First I had to make sure I had a future to worry about.

"You know, you may think you have a killer in custody, but I know he's still out there, and I think I'm still in danger."

"I'll keep a man on you until we actually close this case out," he said. "And by the way, what the hell were you doing leaving your house today?"

"Oh can it," I said, firing right back at him. "I know you have your man watching Julia, not me."

"He's watching all of you."

"Well, I'm actually glad he's there, because my daughter and mother are there, too."

"What?"

"Could you replace him with somebody who shaves?"

"Officer Wilson is a very fine young officer—but, yeah, he is kinda young. I'll see what I can do."

"Thank you."

"What are you going to do now?" he asked.

"I have to go back to Marcy's to get my car, then go back to George's house—"

"Come on, I'll drive you."

I didn't argue. Being in his car with him again meant I got to smell his cologne some more.

By the time we hit the street it was starting to get dark. It didn't seem to me that we'd been in Parker Center and the hospital that long.

"How are things with your boyfriend?" he asked as we got underway.

"Why do you ask?"

"He seemed pretty upset yesterday," Jakes said. "I had a feeling it was aimed more at me than you."

"He's fine," I said. "We're fine."

"Kissed and made up?"

"Yes, not that it's any of your business."

"That's nice," he said, "nice that you patched it up."

"Why do I get the feeling you're being sarcastic?"

"Am I? I get accused of that a lot."

I decided to change the subject.

"Do you really think Andy McIntyre killed Marcy and her husband? Why the husband?"

"I don't know," he said. "That's what our interrogation was supposed to tell us. As for Marcy, we found a draft of a memo in her office recommending that Andy's character be killed off."

"And you think he knew?"

"Why not? Marcy seems like she was that kind of person."

"Well, yeah, she was. . . ."

"And she was trying to get rid of you."

"You find a memo to that effect, too?"

"No, just gossip," he said. "She was, wasn't she?"

"Yes."

"Seems like it was harder for her to get you dumped than McIntyre."

"I don't know. Maybe the stupid bitch thought I had more mileage left on me."

"I think you've got a lot of mileage left on you," he said. "I mean—you don't seem that old—that is, I mean—"

"Stop there, Frank," I said, "and I'll take all the stammering as your attempt to pay me a compliment."

He opened his mouth to say something else, then closed it.

# Chapter 45

When we got to Marcy's Jakes pulled into the driveway and stopped right behind my car. I started to open the door to get out and he put his hand on my arm to stop me.

"Wait."

"For what?"

I wondered if he was going to ask me out.

"Don't open the door."

"Why? Frank, what's going—"

"As we pulled up I thought I saw a flash of light inside."

"Light?"

"Like from a flashlight."

I felt my eyes widen.

"You think there's someone in the house now . . . again?"

"Why don't you just sit here and wait while I find out?"

"Wait." This time I put my hand on his arm. "Don't you want to, like, call for backup or something?"

"I'm just going to check it out," he said. "I don't need backup for that."

"And you want me to wait here?" I asked. "Alone?"

"Don't tell me you're afraid," he said. "You weren't too afraid when you went into the house alone this afternoon."

"Yeah, well, it wasn't dark then, and somebody hadn't already conked me on the head."

"Twice," he reminded me. "Once more and I'm going to have to retire you from the game."

"Okay, I assume that's a sports analogy—"

"Football."

"Not my game. How about I just come with you?"

"Alex—"

"Hey, if all you're doing is checking it out, where's the harm?" I asked.

"You know, you'd make a hell of a cop's girlfriend."

I was taken aback by the comment, momentarily speechless.

"You'd always want to be right in there in every case," he went on, "asking questions every time the guy came home. You're almost like a—"

"Don't say 'buff,'" I cautioned him, holding up my index finger. "I know what that means, and I don't like it."

"Alex," he said, "really I'd be a whole lot more comfortable if you just stayed in the car."

"Are you going to give me a gun?"

"Do you know how to use a gun?"

"No," I said, "I'd probably shoot off a toe."

"Then why—"

"See? I'll be safer with you." I grabbed his arm and squeezed. "Please?"

"I knew the minute I first laid eyes on you. . . ."

"Yes?"

We stared at each other for a long moment. Then he said, "Forget it. Okay, you can come with me, but stay behind me and do what I tell you. Okay?"

"Okay," I said. "Scout's honor. I'll do whatever you tell me."

"Yeah," he said, "that'll happen."

We got out of the car and closed the doors as gently as we could. Then Jakes signaled me to follow him, and he went around to the side of the house with the French doors. Sure enough, they were open.

As he started to go in, I grabbed his arm, put my mouth right to his ear and whispered, "Watch out for the *chachkis*. They'll be all over the place."

He drew away from me, touched his ear, then said, "Turn off your cell, just to be on the safe side."

As a mom I never turn off my cell phone, but I did set it on vibrate.

He went inside and I followed, staying close.

Inside we paused, I assumed, to let our eyes adjust to the darkness. Everything seemed to be as it had been earlier that day. Suddenly, we heard a noise in the back. I couldn't believe that whoever had knocked me on the head late that morning had come back. And that we were here at the same time. I made a note to ask Jakes how big a part coincidence played in his business. It was fascinating.

Jakes put his hand in his jacket, and for some reason I expected him to come out with a flashlight. Instead, he came out with his gun.

We headed down the hallway toward the office and saw that the desk lamp in the back was on. If Jakes had seen a flashlight beam, then whoever it was had probably gotten there only moments before us, used the flashlight to find his way to the office and turned on the desk lamp.

Jakes quickened his step and when we got to the office doorway he said, "Hold it!"

I tried to look past him into the room, but I couldn't see who it was until Jakes moved farther in.

The intruder had frozen where he was, behind the desk.

"I know you," Jakes said.

"Yeah, you do," I said. "That's Thomas Williams, producer of *The Yearning Tide*. Hey, Thomas, I was going to call you in the morning to tell you I won't be at work tomorrow." Wildly inappropriate at the moment, but I didn't know what else to say.

"Somehow," Jakes said, "I don't think Mr. Williams is going to be there, either."

# Chapter 46

We took Thomas back to Parker Center. This time I followed Jakes in my car, while he took Thomas in the backseat of his. He didn't handcuff him, but he did put him in the same interview room where Andy had his heart attack.

"This guy doesn't have a heart condition, does he?" Jakes asked me.

We were watching Thomas through the one-way mirror. He was wearing a dark sweater and jeans, and some kind of sneakers, attire Thomas probably thought a proper burglar would wear.

"Not that I know of. Hey, how come the chief isn't here? And your partner?"

"The chief is home having dinner, hopefully, and so is my partner."

"So you're off duty?"

"I was," Jakes said. "I'm back on the clock now. Tell me about this guy before I go in there and question him."

"He's something of an ass and a poser," I told him. "That said, he's a very good producer."

"What did Marcy's death mean to him?"

"Well, on one hand it made his job harder," I said, "but on the other, he'd already told me he intended to take over her writing duties until someone else could be hired."

"Would this be a move up the food chain for him?" he asked.

"Yes, absolutely," I said. "But I still don't think he did it."

"Let me ask you a question, Alex," Jakes said. "Who do you think killed her?"

"Me? I don't know."

"Well then, how come every time I bring somebody in for it, you say they didn't do it? Come up with an alternative for me. Meanwhile, I'm going in there."

He left and, moments later, entered the interview room. He was right; I kept pooh-poohing every move he made—bringing in Andy, bringing in Thomas—but at least while he was investigating them he wasn't investigating me. But, in all good conscience, I could not believe that either Andy or Thomas had killed Marcy.

There, I said it—or thought it. But if I said it out loud to Jakes, I'd be putting myself on the block again.

Next to the window was a button for an intercom. I pressed it, and Jakes's voice leaped into the room.

"—on, Mr. Williams," he was saying, "you must have had some reason for breaking into Marcy Blanchard's house and ransacking her office."

"I told you," Thomas said. "I didn't break in. I found the side doors open."

"Yes, I know," Jakes said. "I guess she should have put a revolving door in there instead of French doors."

Thomas didn't know what to say to that, so he said something that took no imagination.

"Don't I get a lawyer, or something?"

"You're not under arrest, Mr. Williams," Jakes said. "I could arrest you, though, and then you'd have to call a lawyer. . . ."

"No, no," Thomas said, "I don't need—I didn't do—I was just looking for . . . something."

"Something worth killing for?"

"No!" Thomas said, sharply. "Just . . . something Marcy had that . . . that could be . . ."

"Could be what, Mr. Williams?" Jakes said. "You know, I'm in a rotten mood because I was supposed to be home having dinner right now, like my boss and my partner are. Instead, I'm here dicking around with you. So you better start telling me something that makes sense."

Thomas's shoulders slumped and he said, "All right. Marcy had something that would be . . . embarrassing to me if it fell into the wrong hands."

"Whose wrong hands?"

"The network, the press, you name it."

"So Marcy Blanchard had something on you, but you didn't kill her."

"That's right," Thomas said, "but once she was dead I knew I had to find it."

"So you went to the house this morning, and when Alex surprised you, you hit her on the head and took off."

"Alex?" Thomas looked surprised. "I never—I'd never hit Alex. I—I wasn't at the house this morning, just tonight."

Jakes turned his head and looked at me—well, at the mirror, but it looked like he was looking at me.

"Is Alex all right?" Thomas asked.

"So far."

"I thought she was your prime suspect."

"She isn't, anymore. Somebody tried to kill her two nights ago. They called it a suicide attempt at first, but then they got it right. I'm surprised you didn't read it in the newspaper."

"I did," he said. "I just didn't know that took her off the hook."

"And you read about Andy McIntyre being arrested?" Jakes asked.

"Yes, but that's ridiculous," Thomas said. "Andy wouldn't hurt a fly."

Thomas, I thought, no imagination. But I had to admire the fact that he had regained complete control of himself. You would have thought he was sitting at that table with a staff of writers and not a police detective.

"Are you saying you'd make a better suspect than Andy?"

"I would," Thomas said, "but I didn't do it."

"Wasn't Marcy pushing to get Andy dumped from the show?"

"Yes, she was."

"And you don't think that was motive enough for him to kill her?"

"I'm not saying he didn't have a motive, Lieutenant," Thomas said.

"Detective," Jakes said.

"Detective . . . I'm saying he doesn't have the nerve."

"I see. And you do?"

"Again," Thomas said, "I do, but I didn't."

"Why not?"

"Excuse me?"

"I said, why didn't you kill her if she had something on you?"

"I didn't know where it was," Thomas said, "and killing her wouldn't find it. Then, once she was . . . gone, I figured anyone going through her things might come across it."

"Did you know her ex-husband, Henry Roswell?"

"I'd met him once," Thomas said. "Wait, you said . . . did I know him?"

"He was killed, too. That's been in the paper and on TV."

"Good God, you don't think I had something to do—"

"And why did you wait until now to go to Marcy's house?" Jakes said.

"I—I had to work up the nerve," he said. "I've never done anything like that before."

"You just finished telling me you'd have the nerve to kill somebody," Jakes said. "Now you're telling me you didn't have the nerve to break into her house? Your story is starting to sound a little strange to me, Mr. Williams. I don't know if I want to let you go home tonight."

"Detective," Thomas said, "all I meant was that I have more nerve than Andy McIntyre. Almost anyone would. But whatever I'd do, I'd have to work up to it. There'd have to be good reason."

"And there wasn't good enough reason to kill Marcy?"

"No, there wasn't," Thomas said. "With her alive she was the only one who knew my dirty little secret. With her dead, it could turn up anywhere."

"Okay, Mr. Williams," Jakes said. "Now I'm going to ask you the sixty-four-thousand-dollar question, and if I like the answer I'll let you walk."

"A-all right."

"Just what was this dirty little secret that Marcy knew about?"

# Chapter 47

In the end Jakes allowed Thomas to go home. I made sure he didn't know I was there watching the interrogation. I didn't want Thomas to find out that I knew his secret.

"Let's get you out of here and back to your friend's house," Jakes said.

"I have my car."

"I'll walk you down."

Actually, he had to ride down with me in the elevator to the parking structure, and then walk me to my car.

"It's been a long day," he said.

"Has it ever."

"I'd invite you to dinner, but I think I'm going to go home and collapse until morning."

"I'm sure Wayne'll have something waiting for me when I get back."

"Wayne?"

"He's my friend George's lover, er . . . life partner."

"Ah."

"And he's a hell of a cook."

"Really? Maybe I should wrangle an invite from you, then."

I froze. I didn't know if Paul would be there when I got to George's house, and I certainly didn't want to walk in with Jakes if he was.

"Naw, that's okay," he said, then, taking me off the hook. "Like I said, I'll just go home. . . ."

"And collapse."

"Right."

"Sounds like a good idea."

"Good night, Alex."

"Good night, Frank."

He turned to walk away as I put my key in the door lock, then swiveled back around.

"Although, if I wanted to, say, invite you to dinner another night, uh, what would you say?"

Again, I thought about Paul, and was surprised to hear myself saying, "I think that would be . . . nice."

"No problems with your, uh, boyfriend?"

"Why would there be?" I asked. "It would only be dinner, right?"

"Oh, right," he said, "just dinner, definitely. Like, after the case is over, as a sort of . . . thank-you for your help."

"So I've been helpful?" I asked, playfully.

He hesitated, then said, "Let's just say you haven't been as big a pain in the ass as I thought you'd be, and leave it at that."

"Frank," I said, shaking my head, "sometimes you say the nicest things. . . ."

\*    \*    \*

When I got back to George's house, Paul wasn't there. He had called George and told him he'd tried to get me, but I remembered I had turned my cell off at the last minute before going into Marcy's house with Jakes. I turned it back on later and saw that he'd called, but I hadn't had time to call back.

"I'll give him a call later," I said. "I need a shower. Where's Sarah?"

"She's in her room with Julia. She wanted to stay up till you got home, but for all I know they're both asleep," George said.

"And my mom—," I started, but at that point she came from the kitchen, carrying a cup of tea.

"There you are!" she said. She put the cup down, came at me and wrapped me in a tight hug. "I've been worried sick about you. Where have you been? I thought you were hurt."

Suddenly, she was crying.

"Hey, hey, Mom, I'm fine. . . ."

But there was no consoling her. Suddenly, I realized the full impact all of this was having on my mother.

"I'm sorry, Mom . . . ," I said, and we cried together as Wayne came from the kitchen. Immediately, his eyes got wet.

"It's okay, Mom, it's okay."

I put my arm around her and said to Wayne and George, "I'm going to put her to bed."

Wayne hurried over, picked up my mom's cup of tea and handed it to me. I took both her and the tea into the room we were sharing, closing the door behind us.

"I'm sorry, Alex," she said. "I didn't mean to do

that. I've been trying to put on a brave face, take care of Sarah while you . . . do what you're doing."

"Play detective," I said. "That's what I'm doing, right?"

"Yes," she said, "play detective."

"Look, Mom, I can't—"

She cut me off with a wave of both hands in front of her, as if she were trying to dispel a fog.

"This is not 'the time' for this—I know that," she said, "but when this is over, you should examine your life, look at what this has done to your life, to Sarah's life. Your little girl needs you."

"I know that," I said. "I need her, too."

"Then don't get killed, Alex," she said. "Don't get killed. Remember what I've taught you about priorities? I think you need to examine yours. Now."

She was right and I couldn't think of anything to say.

"I don't want to talk about it anymore," she said. "I'm going to drink my tea and go to bed. Finish what you're doing, and then we'll talk."

"All right, Mom."

"I love you, Alex."

"I love you, too, Mom."

I went back out to the living room. George and Wayne were seated on the sofa. Wayne stood up.

"I'm going to check on the girls and then jump in the shower."

"I'll have dinner waiting for you when you get out," Wayne promised. "I made some chicken marsala. You'll love it."

I was sure I would. No matter what it sounded like, when Wayne cooked it, it was always delicious.

I checked in on the girls and they were awake, but just barely. I gave Sarah a big hug and a kiss, listened while she sleepily told me a story and thought about what my mom had said. I made a point of staying in there, holding Sarah for an extra-long time. I had some thinking to do. I kissed her again and tucked her in.

I went to the other bed and Julia asked, "Have they found the person who killed my parents? I saw on TV that they arrested someone."

"They did, but I don't think he did it. Anyway, he had a heart attack before they could question him, and he's in the hospital."

"He's not the killer?"

"I know him, Julia, and I don't think so. We can talk about it more in the morning."

"Sarah really tired me out today," she said. "She's like the Energizer Bunny."

"I'm sorry," I responded, "it should be me she's tiring out—"

"No, it's okay; I don't mind," she said. "I think I already love her."

"I'm sure she feels the same about you."

Impulsively I leaned down and kissed her forehead and tucked her in.

"Nobody's ever done that for me before," she said sleepily. "It's nice. . . ."

They were both asleep before I left the room.

# Chapter 48

The dinner Wayne had prepared was wonderful. After I checked on my mother and found her asleep, I sat down and ate at the kitchen table. After dinner I touched base with Paul on my cell.

After I finished he was silent.

"Paul?"

"It sounds like you're having the time of your life, Alex," he said.

"Well, I have to admit—"

"You do remember that somebody tried to kill you, right?"

"Well, of course," I said, "but that doesn't mean I'm going to stay cooped up—"

"That's what it should mean," he said. "That you'll stay inside where it's safe until the cops find the killer."

"Paul," I said, "you keep interrupting me—"

"I know. I'm sorry," he said. "I'm worried about you. I couldn't get a hold of you all day and I kept getting . . . bad vibes."

"I'm fine, Paul," I said.

"Don't get hit on the head anymore, okay?"

"I'm going to try not to."

"What's Jakes going to do with poor Andy in the morning?" he asked.

"I don't know," I said. "Drag him downtown if the doctor lets him, I guess."

"And you really don't think Andy or Thomas the producer did it?"

"No," I said, "I can't see it."

"Then who do you like for it?"

"I don't know," I said. "I'm starting to realize how over my head I am."

I waited for him to offer to help. He didn't. He was waiting for me to ask. That was fair. I just had to figure out how. Paul was a resource I'd been wasting.

"Are you going to work tomorrow?"

"I'm not sure."

I wasn't so sure I wanted to see Thomas again, so soon after hearing his great secret.

"I'll decide in the morning. I probably should. I don't want to put the show any further behind schedule."

"Think of your safety first," he advised.

"I will, I promise."

We talked a little more and then we said good night. I looked up from the sofa and saw George watching me.

"What's going on, girl?" he asked.

"With what?"

He came over and sat down.

"Something's going on between you and that detective," he said.

"What makes you say that?"

"I can see it on your face when you talk about him and I can hear it in your voice when you talk to Paul."

"Really?" I asked. "Do you think Paul can hear it?"

"Honey, he's a man," George said. "That means he only hears half of what you say to him, and he's oblivious to the other half."

Wayne came walking in with three glasses of white wine and handed them out.

"This time I'm going to stay and gossip," he said. "What are we talking about?"

"Alex and her men," George said.

"Ooh, the TV guy and the hunky detective."

"Paul's a forensic scientist," I said. "He's not just any TV guy."

"You sound very defensive, missy. I know what you need," Wayne said. Then he looked at George and said, "I know what she needs."

"What?" George and I asked.

"A night out," Wayne said, "with us."

"You want to take me to a bar?"

"Not just any bar, a gay bar." George said. "I think it's a good idea. Some drinking and dancing."

"Girl, you will be adored there," Wayne said, "and you won't have to worry about anybody wanting to have sex with you."

"It'll just be some harmless fun and it'll take your mind off things for a few hours."

I laughed and said, "That does kind of sound like fun. But . . . what about the girls, and Mom?"

"You can put Sarah to bed and we'll go after that. They'll be safe here with the police right outside the door," George said.

"Come on, what do you say?" Wayne asked. "We'll get dressed up and go out on the town tomorrow night."

"Are you going into work tomorrow?" I asked George.

"Honey, I don't get the big bucks the actors get," he said. "I have to go to work. Besides, they'll all look like they're in fright wigs if I don't. But I'll come home early and we'll go out."

"I wasn't sure about going in, but I can call Thomas in the morning and tell him the police don't want me to. Then I can go to the hospital and see what's happening with Andy."

"Doesn't he have any family?"

"No, he doesn't," I said.

"Don't forget his life coach," George said.

"Maybe we should get a life coach," Wayne said to George. "That sounds like fun. Somebody else to make all the decisions for a while."

"We're doing just fine with our lives," George scolded Wayne.

"You're right," Wayne said. "Well, I've got to go do some work before I turn in, so night-night, you two."

He took his wineglass with him into his office.

"What's he working on?" I asked.

"Don't ask me," George said. "He's very secretive about his work. Doesn't like me to see it until it's done. So we're on for tomorrow night?"

"Definitely," I said.

"Good. I'm going to start the dishwasher and then read awhile before I turn in. You have the run of the house."

"I don't know how to thank you, George—"

He patted my hand and said, "Just don't do it every day, hon. Wait until this is all over. Then I'll make you buy me a fattening dinner—which, of course, certain people will know nothing about." He pointed toward Wayne's office.

I put my finger to my lips, drained my glass and gave it to him. He went off to the kitchen and moments later I could hear the humming of the dishwasher.

I got up and walked to the window, looking out to check on our watchdog. Still there. I had my cell in my robe pocket, where I'd put it after hanging up with Paul, and now it vibrated. I picked it up and checked the readout. I was surprised, but pleasantly so.

"Detective," I said, "I thought you were going to collapse."

"I called the hospital just to check on our boy," he said. "Looks like they're going to want to keep him for some more tests."

"Oh, so you won't be able to drag him downtown and frighten him some more."

"Frighten him?" he asked. "I hadn't even got started when he keeled over."

"Okay if I go and visit him at the hospital? He might want to see a friendly face."

"Sure, why not," he said, and then after a long pause added, "I, uh, just might see you there."

"Good night, Frank."

"Night, Alex."

I closed the phone, smiling. I didn't for a minute think he had called just to tell me about Andy.

# Chapter 49

Early the next morning I called Thomas's cell phone and told him I wouldn't be in.

"You'll be putting us behind again, Alex, just when we were about caught up from the whole Marcy . . . thing."

His attitude didn't sound any the worse for wear considering what he had gone through the night before. I wondered how he'd react if I told him I knew everything.

"Thomas, the police don't think I'm safe," I said. "I don't want to endanger everyone else."

"Well, if they'd just catch this killer quick instead of harassing—" He stopped short.

"Yes?"

"Never mind," he said. "We'll tape around you for a few days, Alex."

"Thanks Tho—," I started, but he'd already hung up.

I stared at the phone. If Marcy had dirt on Thomas, who was to say she didn't have dirt on some other people, as well? I knew she didn't have any on me, because there was none to be had. That's what happens when your entire life has been laid bare by the tabloids. I had nothing to hide.

But there were plenty of people connected to the show who did.

After breakfast I headed for the hospital. I didn't bother checking in with our bodyguard. I assumed Jakes would have already called him and warned him about me.

During the drive I thought about Jakes's call the previous night, and also about the way he was feeling me out in the parking lot about dinner. I knew Paul would hit the roof if I went to dinner with Jakes, so why had I indicated that I would?

There was some press still in front of the hospital, but not a lot, and they weren't looking for me any-more. I was able to drive past them into the parking lot and get inside without incident. I knew which room Andy was in, so I took the elevator to his floor and went directly there. A uniformed policeman in his for-ties was standing right at the door, a chair next to him.

"Miss," he said, as I approached.

"Detective Jakes said I could visit Mr. McIntyre," I explained.

"Your name, miss?"

"Alex Peterson," I said, looking at his name tag, "Officer Sorrentino."

"Oh yeah, I got the word that it was okay for you to visit."

"Has Detective Jakes been around yet this morn-ing?" I asked.

"No, Ms. Peterson."

"Thank you."

I went into the room. Andy looked as white as a sheet, with an IV bottle by his bed and tubes in his arm and up his nose. Something was clipped to the end of his finger.

"Hey," I said, approaching the bed.

He turned his head and smiled when he saw me.

"At last," he said. "A friendly face."

"I told Detective Jakes you'd need one, so he let me come in." I leaned over and kissed his cheek. He grabbed my hand.

"Jesus, Alex, I was so scared," he said. "I'm so glad you were there."

"I'm glad I was there, too, Andy."

"Do they really think I killed Marcy?" he asked. "And her ex-husband? Jesus, why would I kill him? Marcy I could see—she was a royal bitch. But I didn't even know him."

"You never met him, Andy?"

"I don't know . . . maybe once. I don't really remember. But I didn't know him well."

"Well, that should work in your favor, then."

"Do you think so?"

"That and the fact that they found Thomas ransacking her house last night."

"What?"

I couldn't help it. It just came pouring out. But I didn't tell Andy what Thomas's secret was. I drew the line there. After all, if neither of them killed Marcy, they'd still have to work together.

"I can't believe it," Andy said when I was done. "I

mean, Thomas would make a better suspect than me, but I don't think he'd kill her."

"Neither do I."

"Well, if you didn't do it and I didn't do it and Thomas didn't do it, who did?"

"I don't know, Andy, but it seems like we're eliminating people, huh?"

Out of nowhere Andy said, "I'll bet it was a woman."

"I've been thinking the same thing, but who? I was the best female suspect they had." I *had* been thinking the same thing, but thought I was grasping at straws. I mean, there was no evidence one way or another, and the person in my garage was a man. So I had nothing to go on but a hunch—and the fact that the men I had been talking to had me believing them, including Andy.

"Marcy must have pissed off all the women who work on the show at one time or another," Andy said.

"I'll bet you're right."

"Alex, are you still asking questions?"

"I'm still poking my nose where it doesn't belong," I told him, "but I'm getting tired of people hitting me on the head."

"What?"

I told him about what happened in my garage, and then again at Marcy's house.

"Are you sure it wasn't Thomas?" he asked. "Either time?"

"Fairly sure," I said. "In my garage I got the impression of someone . . . bulkier."

"That would leave out a woman."

"Unless she has an accomplice."

"I think maybe you better lie low for a while."

"Apparently that's what you're going to do," I said. "They want to do more tests, huh?"

"I don't like being in here," he said, "but I think I prefer it to going to jail. They can run all the tests they want."

The door opened then and we both looked to see who was coming in. It was Jakes.

"Good morning," he said.

"You come to give Andy another heart attack?" I asked. "They haven't finished doing tests after the first one."

Jakes walked to the bed.

"Look, Mr. McIntyre, I'm sorry you had a heart attack. It certainly wasn't my intention—"

"I know that, Detective," Andy said. "You were just doing your job."

"That's right, I was."

"Well, I suppose you'll have to wait until I get out of here to continue doing it."

"I talked with your doctor," Jakes said. "You're safe for a couple more days, but once he cuts you free, I'm afraid we'll have to finish our . . . conversation."

"Could you finish it without being quite so scary?" I asked.

He looked at me with a straight face and said, "I'll see what I can do."

# Chapter 50

I had to admit my amateur investigation was stalled.

My intention had been to go back and talk to everyone I'd questioned the first time around. That meant Andy and Thomas, of course, but in my mind I had already cleared them. There was also Henry Roswell, but he was dead, and Julia, but she was with me now. That left a bunch of people connected to the show: Linda the makeup girl; Amanda, Roman and Lisa, actors with the show; the unhappy director, Sammy . . . and I had never even talked to the writer, Dave Ballwin. Could he be the wild card? But I'd have to go into the studio for that. I'd already called in to cancel my scenes for today, so that would have to wait until tomorrow.

I decided to go back to George's house and spend some much-needed time with Sarah and my mom.

Once again, Jakes walked me to my car.

"I've got to get into work; my partner's waiting," he said, "or I'd buy you a cup of coffee."

I turned and stared at him.

"If I ask you a question, will you tell me the truth?"

"I'll try," he said, "but remember, I'm a cop."

"Is this an act?"

"Is what an act?" he asked.

"This turnaround," I said. "When we first met, and for days after that, I had the distinct feeling you didn't like me. Was that only because you thought I might be a murderer?"

"You want the absolute truth?" he asked.

"That would be a novelty," I said, and almost added, "from a man." But I held my tongue.

"The truth is I liked you from the start, even when I did think you might be a murderer. I thought you were beautiful, intelligent, feisty, all the things I find attractive in a woman. I think you smell good and, if I kissed you right now, I bet you'd taste good, too. Does that answer your questions?"

Answered them and set me back on my heels!

"Well," I said, "all but one."

"And what's that, Alex?"

"Do you even have the slightest doubt now about my innocence?"

"No," he said. "Not the slightest. I don't think you killed either Marcy or her ex-husband. Furthermore, if Andy McIntyre didn't do it, and the killer is out there, I think you're probably still in danger."

"But, why? What possible reason—"

"You'd still look good in the tabloids for this, Alex," he said. "If the killer made one more try at making you look like a suicide, I think people would accept that you did it out of remorse."

"I see."

"So do me a favor," he said. "Keep people around you, and try to stay where my officer can see you and

your family? Stop running around acting like an amateur detective?" He grabbed my arms and for a
moment—one light-headed moment—I thought he
was going to kiss me. Instead he just squeezed and
said, "Stay safe."

Stay safe? That was the best he could do?

"I will," I said. "I promise."

"I'll call you," he said. "We're running down leads
on other people, so—"

"What other people?"

"Go to your friend's house, Alex," he said sternly.

"All right."

"I want to watch you get in your car and lock the
doors."

"Yes, sir!"

I opened my car, got in and locked the doors. He
smiled and waved as I started the car and drove off. I
could see in the rearview mirror that he was still
watching me.

Okay, so I lied again. I decided not to go to
George's, but to go to the studio after all. Today was
the weekly writer's meeting and since I hadn't yet had
a chance to talk to Dave Ballwin, I felt it was a piece of
unfinished business. The last bit of this amateur investigation of mine, and then I would do as my mom said
and examine my priorities.

On the way into work I started thinking about what
Jakes had said. I also thought about how I had told
Paul that we were fine. If we were fine, would I be
standing there, letting Jakes say those things to me?

For a change I got through the front gate without

any awkward moments, despite the fact that I looked nothing like a soap star, that day.

Writers usually did their writing from home, but had to come into the studio for production meetings on occasion. Sure enough Dave was upstairs and the meeting had just ended. He was there with one other person, an old-timer named Ray Williams, who had been writing for soaps as long as there had been soaps. I had heard Marcy say at a meeting once that Ray was hardly relevant anymore, but he had supporters who kept him on the show.

"Hey, Alex," Ray said. "Lookin' . . . relaxed."

"Thanks, Ray."

Given the way I was dressed, he'd been looking for something nice to say, and I thought he'd done a pretty good job.

" 'Scuse me, hon," he said, as he slipped by me, leaving me alone with Dave.

"Hey, Alex," he said.

"Dave." With Marcy gone I had the feeling that Dave would be able to create a decent story line for our resident stud, Roman. Hmm, wouldn't that thought make them good suspects for Jakes? Maybe Dave and Roman planned the murder together? One of them dropped the light as the diversion, and the other one killed her. What I still couldn't figure out was why the same person who killed Marcy would kill her ex. Maybe Henry Roswell's murder was a coincidence, and had been perpetrated by a different person entirely?

"What brings you upstairs?" Dave asked. He did not look anything like Roman Stroud, which is probably why all Marcy stole from him was his talent. He wore thick glasses, carried a backpack and always had a video game with him. He looked like your cliché geek, but was very talented. I'd heard him talking once about a novel he was working on. It was my bet that he'd eventually be a published author.

"Dave," I said, "I wanted to talk to you about Marcy's murder."

He froze at his desk and put down the pages he had been shuffling.

"What about her?"

"I think it's general knowledge around here that she was taking credit for your work."

"That's okay," he said. "She was gonna help me get my novel published."

"That's what she promised you?"

"Yeah."

"And you believed her?"

He looked up at me, his eyes myopic and sad behind the thick lenses, and said, "No," as if the word were being tortured out of him. "I know what she did to Roman. She never kept her promise to him. She was awful, Alex, and I'm glad she's dead."

"Shhh," I said, looking around. "You didn't tell the police that, did you?"

"Of course I did." He swiveled his chair away from his desk and said, "Look at me, Alex. I'm a geek. Who would believe that I could kill somebody?"

Jeffrey Dahmer was a geek; so was Mark David Chapman, but damn it if I didn't believe him. I would never have been able to do Jakes's job. As jaded as I thought I was, I just wasn't able to believe the worst of these people I'd been talking to—people who apparently had been all set to think the worst of me in the days after Marcy's murder.

"Okay, Dave," I said. "Thanks."

He looked at me funny and said, "That's what you wanted?"

I smiled and said, "That was it."

I went down the hall, cut across another one and ended up going by Marcy's office. The door was open and as I went by, I caught a whiff of something familiar. . . . I stuck my head in, and it smelled even stronger. It nagged at me, but I couldn't get it, so I shrugged and left. But the smell followed me. Either that, or it was in the elevator, too.

As I walked to my car I saw Murray the Life Coach getting into his car. He was carrying something, and I assumed that Andy had sent him to pick it up.

"Bye, Alex, see you tonight at the Abbey!"

I looked up and there was Georgie standing on the balcony outside the Hair and Makeup Departments.

"See you tonight! You better get your groove on!" I laughed.

I drove out the gate behind Murray, who waved to the guard. I didn't think he noticed me and that was fine with me. There was no way he and I were ever going to like each other, no matter how much good Andy thought Murray did him.

# Chapter 51

When I got to the house George and Wayne were gone. My mother told me they would meet me at the club. I didn't feel any tension from my mother after our conversation in our room. I guess she really meant it when she said we'd talk after this was all over.

It was a lucky thing I had packed my LBD and my heels when we left my house. After all, how much room does a little black dress take? This one happened to be a favorite of mine, which I wore whenever I wanted to feel or look special. I hadn't been out in a long time, so I decided the best plan was to look good.

When I was ready to go out I modeled for Sarah, Julia and my mother, who all gave me a thumbs-up.

"You look lovely," my mother said.

"You look pretty, Mommy," Sarah said.

Julia smiled at me and said, "Killer."

An unfortunate choice of words, but I accepted the compliment graciously.

I pulled up at the valet at the club called the Abbey that George had told me about. It was a local hangout in West Hollywood where you could get a good martini and some dancing in if you were so inclined. In its day, back, way back, it used to be a church, and the architecture spoke of that. Very moody with lots of brick, and archways draped with deep red velvet. Dripping candles on large, ornate candelabra stood on the terra-cotta tile floors, with all sorts of old religious paintings hanging from the walls. A portrait of irony, I suppose. From church to decadent nightclub.

George and Wayne were already seated at the bar, clutching brightly colored drinks and waving me over.

The very cute and hunky bartender looked at me expectantly.

"Could I get a lemon drop martini, easy on the sugar?"

He walked away and started preparing my drink. I leaned over to George. "That bartender doesn't seem gay."

Wayne piped up. "Probably because he's not. Lots of straight guys tend bar at gay clubs because the money's so good." Who knew?

"Isn't this fun?" George said.

Wayne leaned over and nodded his head toward the end of the bar. "Fun isn't the word."

I followed his gaze and sitting on a bar stool was a beautiful woman. Wait a minute—that woman was not a woman; she was a man! Full makeup, perfectly coifed hair and beautifully manicured nails, wearing a dress tight enough to fool the most discerning eye. Except for the Adam's apple. That gave her/him away. She/he picked up a microphone and shouted, "Welcome to our weekly dance off! We have a lot of great talent lined up for you tonight. Hold on to your hats, boys and girls—here's our first dancer, Jeremy!"

Madonna started blaring from the DJ's booth and Jeremy pranced out onto the small stage directly across from the bar. The music was pounding and George, Wayne and I couldn't help but start moving ourselves. This was fun! I looked over at George and he was covering his eyes and pointing at the stage. Jeremy had started doing a strip of sorts. That got my attention. Not that I'm a perv, but it was fascinating.

"Here's another lemon drop." The bartender slid a martini in front of me. "Courtesy of the two gentlemen over there." He gestured to a couple of guys down the bar who were waving at me and smiling.

"We have loved you forever!" one of them yelled. Well, now isn't that so sweet! Until the other one added, "You are the diva of all divas! You keep it up."

I stifled my speech about divas and smiled, mouthing a thank-you.

The music shifted to Beyoncé and the announcer sitting on the bar introduced another dancer, this time a woman. A real woman. She didn't begin to have the moves that Jeremy had, but she kept her clothes on, gratefully.

The place was really starting to fill up. So much so that we were being pushed closer to the bar than was comfortable. Another guy dancer had taken the stage, kind of a throwback to the Village People construction worker, sans the tool belt and hard hat. The music volume seemed to have been bumped up a notch or five. It was pounding so hard you could feel it in your bones. Something got my attention at the rear of the club. There was a doorway with a red velvet curtain covering it. Standing in front of it was another transvestite, who was staring at me. For a second I thought he was a fan, maybe. But something was off. This guy's gaze was not only penetrating but strangely familiar. And he wouldn't stop staring. His eyes narrowed and then he abruptly disappeared behind the curtain. That was creepy, but before I could give it too much thought George was pulling on my arm.

"I'm getting claustrophobic! I have to go outside," George yelled. "We'll be right back!"

He and Wayne wiggled their way through the now very crowded dance floor toward the exit.

I took another sip of my drink and decided to go to the ladies' room, which turned out to be an experience in itself. It was a toss-up as to who really was a woman and who wasn't, and I wondered how true that was in the men's room. Or was there anyone using the men's room?

When I came out, I turned to go back into the club, but that strange transvestite was standing in the doorway, still glaring at me. There was something awfully familiar about the face beneath the Christina Aguilera wig, and the eyes underneath false eyelashes and peacock blue eye shadow. To finish off the face, "she" had added cotton-candy pink lip gloss. As over-the-top as she was, the hoop earrings she wore were very fashionable. The same could've been said of the blue silk blouse tucked into black capri pants, and the stiletto heels, except that she didn't have the body for it. She seemed comprised more of sharp angles than curves.

Then, just as I got it, I felt somebody bump into me from behind.

"Excuse me—," I said, automatically, but I stopped when I felt something hard poke into my back. And then the smell—that sickly, patchouli smell.

"We're going out the back, Alex," Murray the Life Coach said. "Don't even think about screaming, because then I'll have nothing to lose by firing into the crowd. Do you understand?"

I was frightened and fascinated. I'd never had a gun on me before. I nodded.

"Good," he said, grabbing my left arm, "then let's go."

# Chapter 52

In his car the cloying patchouli smell was even worse. It had been strong in my garage, and then I'd smelled it in Marcy's office earlier that day. Obviously, when I thought Murray was there picking something up for Andy, he was searching Marcy's office. But for what?

"Oh God," he cried out, as if he were in agony, "stop it!"

I wasn't even sure he was talking to me.

"Stop what?"

"Trying to figure it out," he said. "I can hear you in my head."

I looked at the gun he still held in his left hand, pointed at me across his body, while he drove with his right. He was wearing one of those loud shirts he favored, which, inside the darkness of the Abbey, had been hard to make out.

"Murray, you can't blame me for wondering what this is all about."

He took a deep, cleansing breath—I'd seen him do it before—and then he said, "The cosmos reveals all to those who wait, Alex."

I had always thought that Murray the Life Coach

was odd, but until that moment never did I think he
was insane.

"Murray," I said, "I don't think I can wait for the
universe to tell me—"

"Cosmos!" he snapped. "I said cosmos, you stupid
bitch."

"Okay, cosmos," I said. "Look, I'm very nervous because you're pointing that gun at me, so you're either
going to have to shoot me or let me talk." Jesus, did I
really say that?

"Fine," he said, "talk."

"I never even thought about you killing Marcy because I didn't know you had a pass to get on the lot,"
I said. "Not until I saw you there today, and the way
you and the guard exchanged waves."

"Yes," Murray said, "that's Mike. His chakra was in
distress and I helped him. Andy made sure I was able
to come and go as I pleased."

"Great," I said. "So with a pass to get on the lot it
was easy for you to get in and kill Marcy."

"She was trying to get Andy kicked off the show,"
he complained. "Do you know what that would have
done to him?"

I knew what it would have done to Murray's meal
ticket.

"She told him she already had a memo made out to
the network, which she could send in at any time."

"Is that what you were looking for in her office?" I
asked. And then it dawned on me. "That was you at
her house, searching her home office, too."

"You know what I think?" he asked. "I don't think

she ever typed up that memo. She just told poor Andy that to scare him."

And it worked, I thought. Scared Andy, and scared you. Jeez, at that point I hoped Murray couldn't really read minds.

I was also hoping that George and Wayne would have missed me by then, maybe called Jakes to tell him I'd disappeared. They didn't have his phone number, but I was sure if they called 911 they'd connect them to him—wouldn't they?

"And what about Henry Roswell?" I asked. "Why'd you kill him?"

"Him!" he said, spitting the word. "He didn't appreciate what I did for him."

"What did you do for him?"

"I killed his ex-wife."

"I thought you did that for Andy," I said. "To save Andy's job."

"Only until I could relocate."

"Reloc—Wait a minute," I said, getting it, "Henry was your next patsy, wasn't he? Your next meal ticket."

"I could've helped him," Murray said. "I did help him, but he didn't see it that way."

"So you killed him?"

He fell silent, then, maybe afraid he'd already said too much.

"Where are we going, Murray?"

"Don't worry about it."

I looked out the window, studying the passing scenery to try to figure out where he was taking me. Was he still planning to make me look like a suicide?

"You know the police are going to figure this out,

don't you?" I asked. "You left a bloody trail from the Roswell house to Andy's house, which is why they arrested Andy. But once they realize it wasn't him, you'll be the next logical suspect."

"The only logical suspect is going to be you, Alex," Murray said. "It's always been you. You've been trying to influence Andy into getting rid of me since we first met. I don't know what you ever had against me."

"You're a big phony, Murray," I told him. "A charlatan. I could see that from the first moment I met you."

"What makes you so smart?" he asked.

"Maybe having to look out for myself, depend on myself."

Did I really, though? Was I so independent when I had my mother living in the canal house behind me to help out? But I certainly never thought I needed a life coach. A life, maybe, but not a coach.

"So that's why you tried to frame me for killing Marcy?" I asked. "You don't like me?"

"Why not?" he asked. "Your constant bad vibes are constantly fouling up the harmonic frequency of my life. You have no idea how toxic you are."

"And which philosophy did you get that from, Murray?" I asked.

"Shut up, Alex," he said. "You're giving me a headache."

Pretty soon it became apparent where he was taking us. We were headed toward Venice—my house, no doubt, for another suicide attempt, this one to be successful.

# Chapter 53

As he stopped the car in front of my garage and turned off the motor I asked, "Why my house, Murray?"

"Because it's empty," he said.

And where, I thought, do most people commit suicide?

"Murray, the police already know I didn't try to kill myself the other night," I said.

"Get out of the car, slowly."

"Don't you understand?" I asked, opening my door. "This won't work."

He was getting out on his side, still pointing the gun at me across his body. In order to keep the gun on me, he'd have to switch to the outside and point at me over the roof. I wondered if I had the time—or the guts—to duck and run. But the decision was made for me. As I got out of the car, his swollen belly caught on the steering wheel and he couldn't get out with me. By the time he pulled himself free and pointed his gun over the roof, I was gone.

I ducked down as soon as I got out of the car and scooted along the side of the garage. My advantage was twofold—it was dark, and I was on my home ground.

"Come on, Alex," Murray called out. "This won't help. You're only prolonging the inevitable. The end is already preordained."

Murray's phony philosophy seemed to be made up of bits and pieces he stole from many other spiritual practices and teachings. He burned incense; he talked of chakra and chi and things being preordained. I'd heard him speak of Allah and in the next breath mention God. Sometimes I thought he just said the first thing that came into his crazy head.

All of that went through my head in a flash. I think it was my way of trying to keep calm. Murray was still out there. He was bigger and stronger than me, and he had a gun. My heart was pounding as I worked my way behind the building. Unlike most garages, mine didn't have a lot of junk inside or around it. What I wouldn't have given for a stray two-by-four, or a piece of pipe. I thought about using my surfboard, but that just didn't seem practical.

I could have tried to get into my house and maybe grab a knife from the kitchen, but one, could I make it, and two, could I stab somebody, even to save my life?

I decided to go down where my mother's house was, right on the canal, and knock on a neighbor's door. The houses were really close together, and everyone had a communal feeling about the neighborhood. Sure, a neighbor would help me.

It was dark, and the footing could be slippery down there, especially at night, but I saw it as my only chance—unless police cars came blazing down the street any minute—but this was real life.

As I moved away from the garage and crossed the yard, I was glad I hadn't gotten around to stringing those motion sensor lights I'd been thinking about.

I could hear Murray moving around noisily, trying to find his way along the side of the garage. I knew it would only be a matter of time before his eyes adjusted to the dark. Also, there was about a three-quarter moon, which at the moment was behind some clouds. But they were bound to move away soon. I had to get to the canals before that happened.

I started running across the yard, keeping off the concrete part and staying on the grass. As I approached my mother's small house, the grass changed to dirt, so I didn't have to worry about him hearing my footsteps.

"Alex!" Murray called out. "Running to the water won't help."

I was halfway to the water, so I wasn't about to take his word for that.

I quickly went to one of my neighbor's houses and knocked on the door. I didn't yell because I didn't want Murray to hear me. I knocked again, but there must have been no one home. I tried to turn the doorknob, but the door was locked.

I figured I had time to try one more house. I ran to it and knocked on the door. I swore I saw a light inside, but it went off as soon as I knocked. So much for a communal feeling. Okay, maybe that wasn't fair. Who wants to buy into somebody else's trouble? Or maybe it was kids home alone, and they'd been told not to open the door for anyone.

That was it. I had no time to try other houses. I was on my own. No one was going to help me. I had to run for the canals.

Behind the homes along the canals were wooden decks. By keeping to them I'd be able to make my way to one of the bridges.

Right at that moment the clouds moved and the yard was bathed in moonlight. I turned and saw Murray running toward me. With his loud shirt he looked like a beach ball with legs, but he had a gun, so it wasn't very funny.

"Alex! Don't make me shoot!"

"If you shoot me down out here it won't look like a suicide," I called back.

He stopped running and pointed the gun at me. I could hear him panting from the effort, sweat dripping from his face.

"You're not giving me a choice," he said.

We were still thirty feet apart.

"I don't think you can hit me from there," I said, "and too many shots will attract attention."

I hoped I was right and that he wouldn't want to risk having to take more than one shot. He'd want to get a lot closer.

I was betting my life on it.

Suddenly, from the distance, I could hear the sound of police sirens. There was no way of knowing if they were heading for us, but it was sweet music to my ears, anyway.

"Here come the police, Murray," I said. "I guess they figured out where we are."

"Those are fire engines," Murray said, dismissing the sound.

"You can't get away, Alex," he said triumphantly. "There're no police coming, and I don't see any of your neighbors coming out to help you. It's over. Why not just stop and let karma take its course?"

I turned and ran for the water.

# Chapter 54

I'm very comfortable in high heels, I really am. I guess that's why I didn't think to take them off before I started running. But I'm not used to running for my life. The last time I ran in heels it was for a cab. Running from a madman with a gun is different, and I'm sure I wasn't thinking straight.

I made it down to the deck behind my mother's house, then started moving along to the next one. I was going to have to cross several of them before I got to the closest bridge. Right at that moment, though, my heel got caught between two boards and caught me short because there was a strap around my ankle.

I turned, frantically pulling at the heel. Just get the damn thing off, I thought, but before I could, Murray was there, pointing his little gun at me. Funny, but that was the moment I first noticed that it was such a tiny silver-plated automatic, but deadly despite the size.

"Wait, Murray," I said. "I still don't get why you had to kill Henry."

"It started with coffee . . . ," he said, then shook his head. "Ah, I should've known better. I thought we were getting close. . . . I thought I could really help

him. I went to his house that day; told him what I'd
done for him. Do you know what he said to me, the
silly bastard? He still loved Marcy. Still had hope of
getting her back. Can you believe that? He loved that
bitch."

"I guess everybody's got somebody who loves
them, Murray."

"That a dig, Alex? Because I don't?"

"No, Murray—"

"I'd say I'm sorry, Alex," he said, then added, "But
I'm not."

I tensed.

"Hey, hey, hold it there," someone shouted.

We both turned our heads and I saw Paul standing just off the deck, waving his arms. I could see
him clearly because the moonlight was still illumi-
nating everything. And that meant Murray could see
him, too.

"Who is that?" Murray demanded.

"What does it matter, Murray?" I asked. "He's a
witness. You can't shoot me in front of a witness and
call it suicide."

"Put the gun down!" Paul shouted.

"Get away from here!" Murray shouted.

"Just put the gun down," Paul said again, moving a
little closer.

"No, Paul," I shouted, "stay back."

"I can still do this," Murray said, as much to himself
as to me. "All I have to do is get rid of him first."

"Paul—"

Murray turned the gun on Paul, who stopped short

and put his hands up in front of himself. Murray fired and Paul fell back.

"Stop right there!" another voice shouted.

Detective Frank Jakes pointed his gun at Murray, who didn't know what to do, so he made the mistake of pointing his weapon at Jakes, who fired first. I actually saw the bullet strike Murray high on the right shoulder. His little gun fell from his nerveless fingers and he staggered back, falling into the canal.

I ran to the edge as he splashed around, yelling, "Help, help . . . I can't swim. . . ."

I knew those canals were only three to four feet deep, but Murray was in a panic, splashing around.

"Just stand up!" I shouted. "It's only four feet deep."

It was as if he didn't hear me. He continued to struggle and yell. I knew he was shot, and while I hadn't seen him hit his head, he had a gash on his forehead.

"Damn it, Murray." I reached for him, but he was beyond my reach and wasn't doing anything to cut the distance down.

I felt I had no choice. I stepped off the deck into the canal. I also knew the bottom had to be littered with all kinds of junk. Something sucked at my feet and I felt one of my heels go.

I waded over to Murray, who was splashing wildly, and reached for his hand. I grabbed him and tried to pull him to his feet, but he had apparently gotten hooked on something at the bottom and I wasn't strong enough to pull him free. He hit me in the chest, completely by accident, but the impact knocked me over and I went down. By the time I got to my feet, sputtering and trying to get my wet hair out of my eyes, he was gone.

"Alex . . ."

I felt strong hands grab me from behind and pull me out of the water. At the same time I saw Detective Davis go into the canal and wade over to where Murray had sunk from sight.

"Are you all right?" Jakes asked.

"Yes," I said, feeling dazed, "yes, I'm fine. But I—I don't understand. The water's only four feet deep. How could he—"

I looked past him and saw Paul standing with one hand clasped over the other arm. There was blood coming from between his fingers.

"Paul," I yelled, and went to him. "Are you all right?"

"I'm okay, Alex," he said.

"That was stupid," I said. "You had no weapon."

"I had to do something," Paul said. "I couldn't just stand there and watch him shoot you, could I?"

"No, and I'm glad you couldn't."

We both looked over at the canal, where Jakes had gone into the water to help his partner find Murray.

We waited inside the house while they tried to locate Murray. A crew came to drag the canal, and they erected enough lights to make it seem like daytime. Jakes had found a blanket and wrapped it around me, almost tenderly.

An ambulance came and treated Paul's wound, which was in the left bicep. It would hurt for a while, but it was a small-caliber bullet and there wouldn't be any lasting damage.

People started to arrive after that—George and Wayne, with my mother, Sarah and Julia.

# Chapter 55

"Can I sleep in my bed, Mommy?" Sarah asked me, sleepily.

"Of course you can, darling."

"I'll take her," Julia said. She paused a moment, then asked me, "Did you get him, Alex?"

"We got him, hon."

She hesitated a moment, then nodded, picked up Sarah and carried her to her room.

"By the way, your manager, Connie? She's been trying to reach you all day. She said this time it's a really good one."

"I'm certainly not in the mood for any of that," I told Julia as I started to walk away.

I found out that the transvestite I had seen in the Abbey was, indeed, my producer, Thomas. That was the big secret that Marcy had somehow found out. She must have told him—as she had told Andy—that she'd written it in a memo; otherwise why would he have been searching her home office?

"He came over and told us that Murray had taken you out the back door," George explained.

"We didn't know what to do, so I called nine-one-one and George called Paul."

"How did you have Paul's number?" I asked George.

"Hello?" he said. "Four-one-one?"

"You remembered his last name?"

"I remember everything you tell me, doll."

Paul came over, his arm in a sling, and said, "They want to take me to the hospital, just to be sure."

I reached my hand up to take his good one and squeezed it.

"I still need to do some things here," I told him. "If they keep you overnight I'll come by and see you in the morning."

"I'll call you and let you know what happens," he promised. He leaned over and kissed me, and then went off with the ambulance crew.

Slowly the crowd started to dwindle. Paul was gone; George and Wayne left; Sarah and Julia were in bed. My mother wanted to go to her own bed, but couldn't while all those lights were on by the canal, so she went to the sofa.

I walked out the back to watch as they dragged the canal. It wasn't that deep or that wide, so I figured they'd have to come up with the body sooner or later. Then I noticed some commotion and heard yelling; Jakes came walking up to me while his partner stayed down by the action.

"Did they find him?"

"They found him," Jakes said. "They had to untangle him from some crap at the bottom."

"So it's really over?" I said. "He killed Marcy and Henry?"

"Apparently," Jakes said, "although you're the only one who talked to him tonight. What did he have to say?"

I told him about the memo Marcy might have written about Andy, and how that would have killed Murray's meal ticket.

"And do you think Marcy really wrote that memo?" he asked.

"She was mean enough to have made the whole thing up," I said.

"Which means two people died for nothing. Although . . ."

"Although what?"

"Well, from everything we learned about Marcy Blanchard," he said, "she was mean enough that someone probably would have killed her sooner or later."

"I suppose. . . ."

"Well," he said, turning to look out at the canal, where they were bringing up Murray's body, "he was real high on our list once we found out his real name."

"All I ever knew him as was Murray the Life Coach."

"Well, Murray the Life Coach had tried this dodge on different people under different names. He was a con artist named Willie Bendix. He'd latch on to somebody with money, shmooze them with a bunch of religious or metaphysical crap and take them for a ride. When the money was gone, so was he."

"I figured he was a phony from the start," I said. "I tried to warn Andy."

"I guess he figured to ride a soap star like Andy McIntyre for a while."

"And Marcy threatened that."

"It didn't figure he'd turn to murder," Jakes said. "Who knew?"

"So if he was high on your list, why weren't you watching him?"

"We were," he said. "He got away from us tonight. How did he find you?"

"Murray had been at the studio earlier in the day, as I had. He must have overheard George yelling to me in the parking lot about meeting at the Abbey," I said.

"Well, either that or he followed you. Either way, he found you. What did he tell you about Henry Roswell?"

I explained how he thought he was doing Henry a favor by killing Marcy.

"Did he tell you how he met Henry? How he decided that Roswell was his next meal ticket?"

"He started to ramble at that point," I answered. "Something about thinking they were getting close."

"The problem with cases like this," Jakes said, "is you don't always come up with all the answers, even after the case is closed. You have to catch the killer alive, and even then he may not tell you everything."

"Like what?"

"Well, just for closure I'd like to have a definite connection between Murray and Henry Roswell. I mean, other than the fact that they lived down the beach from each other."

I turned to look at him, pulling the blanket closer around me.

"I may have that for you."

"What do you mean?"

"Coffee . . . ," I said, remembering. "He said it started with coffee. . . ."

"What?"

"When I went to talk to Andy, he had Murray make me some coffee," I said. "It was a special blend he got from some coffee place across town."

"So?"

"So when I made coffee at the Roswell house that day, it was the same coffee, from the same shop." I was getting excited that I had the connection the police probably never would have found.

"A shop across town?"

I nodded.

"Jesus . . . ," he said, rubbing his jaw. "Wouldn't it be a hoot if that's where they met, before Murray even *knew* Henry was married to Marcy?"

"How often do you come up with a coincidence like that in your business, Detective?"

"More than you'd think," he said. "Thank you, Alex. I'll take a ride over to that shop tomorrow, see how many people use that same special blend, show them photos of Murray and Henry and see what's what."

"Something still bothers me," I said.

"What?"

"The light," I said, "the one that fell at the studio. How did he work that? I can't believe he went up on the catwalk, dropped it and got to Marcy's office so fast."

"We checked that out," he said. "You don't have to go up on any catwalk. The lights are lowered from the floor, back in the dark. We checked them all and found that a bolt had been loosened so that it would eventually fall out. All he had to do was wait for his chance."

"He had that much patience and knowledge of how things worked?"

"Apparently."

"I have another question."

He looked at me.

"How did you know to come here? For that matter, how did Paul?"

"Your friend George's partner—Wayne?—tried to get me through nine-one-one, but he had a problem getting connected to me. So when George got through to your boyfriend, he called me. There was no way we could know for sure where Murray was taking you, but I thought if he was going to try the suicide dodge again, he'd probably bring you here, where he knew it was empty and safe. So Paul and I agreed to meet here. He arrived first."

"Too bad for him—he got shot for it."

"It's good for you he got here when he did," Jakes added. "He distracted Murray long enough for me to take my shot."

"So I guess you're both my heroes," I said.

"I suppose." He didn't look happy about having to share the role.

They carried Murray's bagged body past us, and all

the cops followed. Davis, bringing up the rear, said, "Good night, Alex. See you on TV."

"Is he really a fan of the show, or was that an act?" I asked.

"Oh, no," Jakes said. "He's a definite fanatic about Tiffany."

"And you?" I asked.

"I don't know Tiffany," he said, "but I think I could get to be a fanatic about Alex Peterson, if I'm given the chance."

He grabbed me then, by the front of the blanket, as I'd been thinking—or hoping—he would all along. He pulled me to him and kissed me. I melted into it for a minute—a long minute—and then pushed away, but not all that convincingly.

He smiled, seemed to wait for the slap that never came, and said, "I'll see you around, Alex."

"Alex! Alex! This way!"

"No, this way Alex, your left!"

"Over here, Alex!"

"Great dress, Alexis. Who are you wearing?"

I exited the limo, making sure not to flash anyone. Just then a crowd of fans caught sight of me and burst into screams.

"Alex, we love you! We love you! Why did you leave *The Yearning Tide*?"

Why did I leave? How could I stay with a show where the whole cast and crew had believed that I murdered the head writer? Could you work with a bunch of people who thought you were capable of that?

As I turned and smiled I was assaulted by a multitude of flashbulbs exploding in my face. My manager, Connie, grabbed my elbow and steered me past the paparazzi.

"Al, *Entertainment Tonight* wants to talk to you, right up ahead."

"Okay, Connie, loosen the death grip, will ya?" I felt a drop of sweat traveling from between my shoulder blades down to the small of my back.

"God, why is it always so hot at the Daytime Emmys? I'm dying!" My perfectly made-up face was quickly disintegrating.

"You look great, doll. Just do your thing!"

A large microphone with the letters *ET* was thrust in my face.

"Alexis, thanks for talking with us. So, how does it feel to be here tonight representing a different show?"

"It's so great. I'm having so much fun. The cast and crew of *The Bare and the Brazen* are so terrific. And you know, after all the drama of last year, it's nice to make a fresh start!"

"We understand you'll be presenting the Best Supporting Actor Award with Jackson Masters. Now, that's a hunk!"

"Yes, and I'm very excited about it. Jackson's a sweetheart."

"Thanks so much for talking to us, Alexis. You look amazing! Who are you wearing?"

Before I could answer or say thank you the mike was quickly whisked away from my face and shoved into the more in-demand face of Ellen DeGeneres. "Ellen, you look amazing tonight. . . ."

Connie's gravelly voice cut through the wall of noise.

"By the way, Al, the stage manager asked me if you'd seen Jackson Masters. He never showed up for rehearsal."

"No, I haven't. But Jackson always blows off

rehearsals. He'll probably run up there at the last minute. He loves to jerk my chain."

I proceeded up the steps to the Kodak Theatre and took a deep breath. Bells were ringing, letting everyone know the show was about to start.

"Please take your seats, everyone, we start in five minutes! Five minutes everyone!" came blasting over the PA system.

The Kodak Theatre was a fairly new award venue. It was part of a very large and very expensive attempt to overhaul Hollywood Boulevard. They had done a good job. There were many floors with bars and restaurants and shops connected to the theater.

I gingerly walked down the aisle, being careful not to trip on my train, and found my seat in the front row.

"Hi, Elmo!" Now that was exciting. Elmo and Grover from *Sesame Street* were sitting in my row! I had to get a photo. My four-year-old daughter, Sarah, would be in awe!

"Hey, Alex!" I looked over and saw Lisa Daley smiling at me from *The Yearning Tide* section.

"Hey, Lisa! How are you?" Lisa was one of the few people on the *Tide* who had remained my friend after I left the show. A few of the other actors on the show glanced at me, then guiltily looked away. Good, you should feel guilty, you lousy bastards! I thought. Those people were so quick to believe I could commit murder.

"Take your seats, people. We are counting down to live television! One minute. *One minute!*"

The stage manager ran up to me.

"Ms. Peterson, could you please come backstage

and get ready to present? Have you seen Mr. Masters?"

"No, I haven't. You still haven't found him?"

I looked around and didn't see him anywhere. We were presenting the first award! This was cutting it close even for Jackson. I grabbed my train and hustled backstage. There was a lot of commotion. Hair and Makeup grabbed me and gave me the once-over with powder and hairspray.

There was a mad dash for any stragglers to take their seats. And suddenly a loud explosion of music enveloped the stage.

"Thirty seconds . . . twenty seconds . . . ten, nine, eight, seven, six, five, four, three and we are live!"

I've often wondered why they bothered counting down when they never seemed to get to number one.

"Welcome to the thirty-ninth annual Daytime Emmy Awards, hosted by Melody Thomas Scott and Peter Bergman!" Thunderous applause erupted for the two stars of *The Young and the Restless*.

There must have been a thousand fans seated in the upper balconies, and as Melody and Peter walked onto the stage, they all erupted into cheers and applause.

"Welcome. Tonight is going to be an exciting evening, isn't it Peter?"

"Yes, Melody, it is. And it is my pleasure to be hosting this illustrious event with someone as charming as you."

"Oh, thank you, Peter! I'm so excited about tonight's show! The finest in daytime television are here. All the talk shows, game shows, children's shows, and, of course, the best of the best in daytime dramas are represented!"

"Well, then, let's get to it, Melody!"

"Yes, let's! Our first presenters are one hot couple. She's proven that forty really is the new twenty! And if that's true, then he's proof that twenty must be the new embryo! From *The Bare and the Brazen*, it's two-time Emmy winner Alexis Peterson and gorgeous newcomer Jackson Masters!"

Who wrote this crap, anyway? I hesitated. I mean, should I go without Jackson or what? I looked at the stage manager questioningly. The producer of the event, Dick Clark, ran up to me.

"Alexis! Just go without him. Make sure to read his part off the cue cards. Can you do that?"

"Yeah, Dick, of course . . . I'll do my best."

I stepped onto the stage and into the mouth of this huge theater. An explosive burst of applause and screams greeted me. It took every fiber of my being not to trip on my freaking train. Why did I wear this stupid dress? I hate trains!

"Good evening! I'm here to present the award for best supporting actor." I looked behind me one last time. No Jackson. "Unfortunately, my costar is nowhere to be found! Probably somewhere doing some pushups, ha ha! You think he was born with that six-pack?" Not so great, but the best I could come up with on the spur of the moment. Give me a break! I was thinking on my feet! I quickly looked at the next cue card and read Jackson's lines.

"The nominees for Best Supporting Actor are . . . Jamie Martin, *The Best Days Are Ahead*." I paused when they ran quick clips of each actor's work. "Thad Weber, *The Depths of the Sea* . . . Don Duncan, *The Tears of Tomorrow* . . . Roman Stroud, *The Yearning Tide* . . . and Vance McKenzie, *Too Late for Yesterday.*"

As I began to open the envelope I felt something drip on my nose. I knew I was sweaty, but this was ridiculous! I quickly brushed off my nose with my fingertips. Weird; they were red. I looked at them quizzically until it registered. It was blood! I looked up and something was hanging in the rafters far above the stage. Slowly my mind wrapped around what I was looking at. It was a body!

And a dead one at that.

Just then the body disengaged from whatever it was hanging on and fell several feet. It was poised in midair, still attached to a chain, slowly spinning around and around.

Right next to me.

Right where Jackson was supposed to be. I looked at the distorted and bloodied face.

And then I realized.

It *was* Jackson!

# Penguin Group (USA) Online

*What will you be reading tomorrow?*

Tom Clancy, Patricia Cornwell, W.E.B. Griffin,
Nora Roberts, William Gibson, Robin Cook,
Brian Jacques, Catherine Coulter, Stephen King,
Dean Koontz, Ken Follett, Clive Cussler,
Eric Jerome Dickey, John Sandford,
Terry McMillan, Sue Monk Kidd, Amy Tan,
John Berendt…

You'll find them all at
**penguin.com**

*Read excerpts and newsletters,*
*find tour schedules and reading group guides,*
*and enter contests.*

Subscribe to Penguin Group (USA) newsletters
and get an exclusive inside look
at exciting new titles and the authors you love
long before everyone else does.

**PENGUIN GROUP (USA)**
us.penguingroup.com